FALLEN
A SINFUL SOLDIER ROMANCE

LEXXI JAMES

CHAPTER 1

KATHRYN

Kathryn sat on a buttery-soft leather couch in the office of Mr. Paco Robles, giving him more than a once-over. Across from her sat the right-hand man to the CEO of Drake Global Industries, hiding so many secrets, she wondered just how many he held in that handsome head of his.

They were kindred spirits from the start, during her worst interview ever, when he'd become a last-minute stand-in as her interviewer for an investigative position in insurance fraud with Wolff Investigations, a close partner of Drake Global Industries. Half intending to blow her chances, she'd proclaimed herself a washed-up ER nurse needing a change of pace.

Despite his immaculate attire and unmistakable wealth, Paco had been casual and kind as he asked her a litany of questions, eventually exposing the pain in her heart. And very quickly, she'd understood.

They were one and the same.

Kathryn had gotten the job, and they'd been close in the three years since. But today, she rolled the dice on testing the depths of their friendship. No, she wasn't sizing him up for a baby-daddy proposition or anything. If only it were that easy.

Somehow, as they brainstormed over the perplexing particulars of her latest case, his innocently asking, "How have you been?" gave her an invitation to spill her deepest, darkest needs.

Then again, it's Paco. Obvious case of voodoo.

His question was warm, sincere, and rather ordinary in the moment. The man literally asked how she was doing. But he was here. In Colorado. And the opportunity was too good. It wasn't until she heard her own insane words aloud that she realized the extent of his black-magic truth spell.

"Paco," she asked, "how much do you know about BDSM?"

As quick as a whip, he charmed her with a smile and blurted out his standard response to any question that started with "How much do you know about . . ." You could fill in the blank with almost anything, and his answer would always be the same.

"Enough to be dangerous," he answered confidently.

But he was more than a friend. She trusted him. There weren't many who made that cut, and fewer that she'd let in on the lascivious lockbox of her soul. Besides, it was Paco, tough as nails with a soft side. Like her, he hid his heartbreak behind his smile, and would do anything for a friend. Or almost anything.

Asking him for a favor seemed harmless enough at the time.

"Listen, I'm becoming . . . curious." Her statement came out more like a question, and his smile just egged her on. "Maybe, you could, um, *show* me what you know?"

"Kathryn, I'm flattered, and honored, that you'd want me to help you through this journey. But, and maybe I'm slipping in exuding the right aura . . . I'm gay."

"And that makes this even more perfect." The unmistakable confusion on his face prompted her to explain. "I'm just learning the ropes. Literally, right? And I don't even know if this is something I really want or will like. And without a doubt, I don't want to muddle my emotions with s-e-x. I'm going in scientifically. From a . . . clinical perspective."

His eyebrows rose, clearly shouting *bullshit* without a word.

Kathryn sighed. "Fine. I admit, I'm not really sure what I want. Maybe just to explore a little."

"Or a lot?"

She huffed out a laugh. "Or a lot."

Grinning, he stood and scooped her up into a bear hug, dropping the sweetest kiss to her temple.

"Paternal head kiss," she mumbled against his chest. "It's the nicest letdown I've ever had."

Without letting go, he squeezed tighter. "I hope you know me better than that. I don't do disappointment. I find workarounds. And, Ms. Kathryn Chase, I'd like to propose one hell of a counteroffer."

CHAPTER 2

JAKE

Relieved to tear his gaze away from the strain of his computer screen, Jake Russo smiled for the first time that day. Seeing the Caller ID pop up was just the excuse he needed to escape the virtual hamster wheel of chasing lines of code.

Like a kid, he shoved his executive chair away from his desk, rolling back, and answered as it swiveled to a stop. "Mr. Paco Robles. What Pandora's box have I just opened by picking up your call?" Eager for the distraction, he shoved away his twinge of suspicion.

"One that I'd rather discuss in person. How about a drink? I'll buy."

Music to my ears.

Wherever Paco went, excitement followed. He did a great job of hiding the dirt beneath the nails of his perfectly manicured hands. His real job remained a mystery, but one thing was for certain.

No one had ever accused the man of being boring.

Ready to kick his snooze-fest of a day in the balls, Jake

embraced the suggestion. An adrenaline rush was headed his way, and God, did he need one.

His laugh echoed off the walls of his large home office, bouncing off the floor-to-ceiling windows overlooking the bright Colorado mountains. "Haven't you ever heard there's no such thing as a free drink? I'm pretty sure that saying originated because of you."

Paco's chuckle was casual. "Well, if it'll ease your mind, you can buy the drinks. You're gonna need one for this conversation."

So they required privacy. Unsaid, but understood.

"Sure," Jake said. "I can be in New York in a few hours."

"As a matter of fact, I'm in town."

"How convenient." Unsurprised, Jake rolled with it. "My place? You haven't seen the new digs. And you're welcome to crash here if you're sticking around."

"I'm taking off tonight, though I appreciate the offer. But your place it is."

The words barely had a second to push through the speaker phone when Jake's security system pinged, announcing a visitor. The sensor alerted him of movement at the tall iron gate protecting the entry of his mile-long driveway. He clicked over to the camera's live feed.

Free of any actions from him, the gate opened. Paco slipped his arm back into the car, having just swiped a card across the security panel.

"Seriously, man," Jake grumbled. "You give new meaning to the term *all-access pass*."

"The perks of your house doubling as a headquarters. As if you don't slip in and out of places on a whim. You just do it in cyberspace."

Amused, Jake smirked. "No comment."

Normally, Jake would enjoy the social graces of giving Paco a full tour of the house with a double scoop of small talk, but this wasn't the time. As Jake opened the front door and ushered Paco inside, he detected something brewing behind his guest's normal poker face.

"Okay, Mr. Robles, we'll get down to business in a minute. But the important stuff first. Let me present you with our full drink menu. Whiskey neat. Whiskey with water. Whiskey on the rocks."

Paco nodded at the assorted bottles of Jake's favorite liquor. "I'll take whatever you're having, but I need a glass of pure Rocky Mountain tap water too. The altitude hits me hard if I don't stay hydrated."

"Coming up."

As Jake poured their drinks, Paco cut to the chase. "Two things. First, a case is about to cross your path."

"Sure, what is it?"

Hesitating, Paco shook his head. "Nope. We all agreed. Because of the players and the unique opportunity the situation presents, it needs to unravel for you. We're staying out of it."

"Who's *we*? You and Alex?" Alex Drake, the *Drake* of Drake Global Industries.

Jake and Alex knew each other casually, though the man always managed to check on him without intruding.

"And Mark."

My boss? "Hold up. You've got to give me more than *the universe will bring you a case*."

"Oh, we might puppet-master the universe a smidge, but the case was headed your way with or without us. And we're all keenly interested. But that's all I can share right now."

Jake gave him the hairy eyeball.

Smirking, Paco averted his gaze, winding up to throw him a fast one. "Let's change the subject. Are you seeing anyone?"

He's got to be kidding.

Jake's head dropped, heavy with the weight of disinterest. "No. And *no*."

When Paco responded with a popped brow, Jake tossed back the rest of his shot rather than drag out the conversation with leisurely sipping. "Sorry you wasted a trip if matchmaking was on your mind."

Undeterred, Paco took his lowball in one hand, his water in the other, and made a leisurely stride to the rustic leather sofa in the great room. He sat, making himself at home with a broad cheesy grin.

Jake grabbed his own water before reluctantly shuffling over. "You're fucking worse than my mother, you know that?"

"I love Grace. How are your folks doing?"

"Great. Had you been here a few days ago, the two of you could've tag teamed. Picked my wardrobe, cosmos overflowing, and swiping right all over the damn place."

Paco chuckled, and Jake joined him.

"Well," Paco said drolly, "there are things I know about you that Grace definitely does not."

Fair enough.

Jake breathed through the candid conversation, presented with a clearer picture of where Paco was going. "That was years ago."

Paco sipped, then eyed the amber liquid sliding down the inside walls of his glass as he gave it a gentle swirl. "So, it was just something you did, and not who you are?" His gaze shot to Jake.

Jake swallowed whatever lie he'd teed up. Lying to Paco was like lying to his own reflection. What was the point? "Too much has happened since then."

Paco's nod was heavy with understanding. "Trust me. I get it. Casual one-nighters fill the void, but the reality is that it's easier to avoid relationships than settle for half a life." When Jake rolled his eyes with a cautious grin, Paco gave him a serious look. "Listen to your elder on this one. I've been single for ten years because faking it isn't my style. I need to be fulfilled. Accepted for all I am. Dirty hands, kinks, and all."

"Fuck." Jake huffed out the curse with a smile. "If this is your idea of a pep talk, you've got some serious room for improvement."

Paco held up a hand. "Let me finish. I know where you're coming from, and I'm not judging. You have a chance to tear out of that cocoon you've built around yourself."

"There's safety in a cocoon. And not just for me." Jake gave his head a slow shake. "I lost half my team. I should've died myself. Doms can't have anger management issues. Look at me—it's been years, and I never know what's going to set me off."

"And I get it. Valid point."

"But?"

"But . . ." Paco blew out a breath, staring at the liquid he swirled in his glass. "I've got a friend. A close friend. She's . . . looking for something. I can't give her the kind of help she needs, but you can. Let's just say she's been bottling herself up in a way that worries me. Like, any day now, she'll crack and be impulsive because she's under so much pressure, she's about to explode. I know her. She'll hit the gas hard, blow right past her caution and common sense, and throw her vulnerabilities into the hands of whoever binds them. Jump on Craigslist or some crazy shit like that."

Jake frowned. "So, what? Your friend needs a list of safe places she can try?"

"She won't go for it, for two reasons. One, like you, she's insanely private, almost reclusive nowadays. Thank God she's got a small group of trusted friends, or she'd never get out. A few years back, her world changed." Paco paused, giving Jake a knowing look. "She's going through the motions day in and day out, but now she wonders if some of what she needs is to slip into submission. And she has no idea what she's looking for. She needs a safe way to explore. Someone who will push her boundaries without breaking her. Really understand her from the inside out."

Listening intently, Jake knew Paco wouldn't be involving him unless it was in some bizarre way important. "I'm intrigued, but still not sure I'm entirely interested. It's a relationship. At least, it should be. I'm not exactly on the Dom-for-pay market."

Paco shook his head. "No problem, because she's not looking for that. Just as she's not exactly looking for love. So much so, she has a teensy little hard limit. But just one." He chuckled as he lifted the whiskey back to his lips. "No sex," he said, pouring the last of his drink through his smiling lips.

Jake scoffed. "I'm a Dom, not a monk. I think you're confused about which lifestyle I gave up. I assure you, that wasn't it."

"Think of it as her way of making you earn her trust."

"And that's the issue. There's no relationship to earn trust from. Punishing a sub is only half the role. Doms are here for the rewards too. Funishment. Pleasure. Sorry, man. Her hard limit is my hard pass."

Paco caved. "You're probably right. It's a lot to ask, but like I said, I had to try." He stood, buttoning his perfectly tailored navy blazer, and headed for the door as he added nonchalantly, "With it being Kathryn Chase and all."

Jake jumped in front of the man, blown away by the grenade just tossed between them. "Wait. I'll do it. Where? When?"

Paco cocked his head. "What? Now you're interested? Well, I guess that makes sense . . . since you've been on-again, off-again stalking her for years."

Defensive, Jake sank back on the couch. "It's not like that, and you know it. She lost her job, and maybe herself, all because of me. I've just been keeping tabs on her to make sure she's all right. I didn't want to interfere with her putting her life back together. Who knows how she'd react to seeing me. I . . ." He hung his head, letting his words trail off. "But I'd do anything for her. Anything."

Paco's hand landed firmly on his shoulder, and he met Jake's troubled gaze with assurance. "I know. Like I know with every fiber of my being that you'd never harm a hair on her sweet head. I have faith in you, maybe more than you have in yourself. There aren't many people I'd trust with my life, and fewer that I'd trust with hers. You know the consequences if she ventures out in the wrong hands."

A serious silence hung between them.

Contemplating the statement, panic focused Jake. "Tell her you've got just the Dom."

"Good. I'll set everything up. Sometime soon."

"But to do this right, she has to be unrestrained in the moment. Willing to let go of everything she's holding back. At least for our first meeting, she can't know it's me."

Paco's face filled with intrigue. "What are you gonna do, dress up like Zorro?"

Jake chuckled. "If she's into it, next time. But I had something more traditional in mind."

CHAPTER 3

KATHRYN

At nearly seven p.m., Kathryn came to terms with the truth. *I'm out of my damn mind.* A few short weeks ago, her secret rendezvous seemed eons away. A blink later, and her trusted confidant Paco was escorting her into the palatial presidential suite of the Denver Four Seasons Hotel.

The grandeur of the suite had her questioning too many decisions in her life. Career choice. Casual wardrobe selection. The adolescent statement of a ponytail high on her head. The ridiculous amount of trust she had in a suave Puerto Rican charmer who promised seduction and sanity on a silver platter.

Hence, why she now sat on the edge of a plush bed that looked way too pretty for butt prints. Once he'd left, she'd slid on the soft satin blindfold as she'd been instructed. Her simple light-blue blouse was offset by a classic black skirt, which let an errant breeze cool her thighs and whisper against her lacy panties.

Even in her lightly padded bra, her nipples were doing their damnedest to bust free from the chill. Apprehensive, she tried not to fidget as the minutes dragged out, letting too many thoughts bombard her mind.

What will my Dom be like? Or the *Dom. Obviously, he's not my Dom. I don't even know his name.*

As she started to shiver, she found her patience wearing thin.

I should just leave. Paco said I could leave anytime before . . . or during. During what?

A determined sigh blew past her lips as she tugged a corner of the comforter free to cover her lap.

Okay, fine. I'm not leaving. She kicked off the heels that squeezed a little tighter than they did in the store less than an hour ago, cementing her stay.

She'd almost forgiven her Latino benefactor for putting the kibosh on the minibar, insisting that this experience had to be one hundred percent sober. Without a cocktail to take the edge off, she barely kept her freak-out under control.

Wondering why she sat waiting wasn't useful.

I know exactly why I'm here.

CHAPTER 4

KATHRYN

Three years earlier – Middle East

"Clear!" Kathryn barked, and all hands ripped away from the soldier's battered body.

The defibrillator paddles sent an electrical charge that contorted his back to an arch. A second later, his body crashed back on the gurney, the electric zap having run through the lifeless man.

One thousand volts.

The dial had been turned up for each of the three attempts. That meant it was maxed out, and by standard operating procedures, they were done. Not much more to do but call the time of death.

Not this time.

This would be her fifth loss in a row as an Army trauma nurse.

From the barely climate-controlled tent in the heart of the Middle East, Captain Kathryn Chase wasn't headed for a breakdown. She'd snapped about thirty seconds ago, and protocol was about to be her bitch.

I'm not a fucking robot.

The colonel peeled off his surgical gloves, reciting as the attending physician what would be the final record for the recently departed. "Sergeant First Class Russo. Time of death—"

"No!" Kathryn shouted.

What could she do?

The defibrillator was out. Areas without bullet holes now had fresh paddle burns from the series of jolts.

Instinctively, she locked her arms and pressed the heel of her hand over and over into his chest. For a nurse determined not to give up, cardiopulmonary resuscitation, or CPR, was her last option.

A technician gingerly touched her arm, urging her to stop. But Kathryn shoved the corporal back hard enough to knock over several rolling trays of mobile equipment. She hadn't meant to, but she was . . .

Focused.

Determined.

Obsessed.

Under her breath, she huffed, "One, two, three, four, five," counting the compressions as she looped the phrase over and over again.

The colonel took a different approach, persuading her with a stern command. "Captain Chase."

I can't stop. I won't.

Reaching across the patient's body, the colonel grabbed her arms, halting her compressions. "Kathryn," he said, his voice solemn and coaxing. "It's time."

Unable to control herself, she sobbed, choking in an attempt to hold it back. Defeated, she shut her eyes, her exhausted body collapsing on the patient as her flood of tears coated his skin.

As she bawled uncontrollably, something she'd never done in public in her professional career, everything slowed. She heard every sound. The whispers of the staff working around her. The mechanical blips of the medical machinery. The swishing of a hand gently rubbing her back. Her own voice uncontrollably heaving *no*.

Then there was another noise, one that made her pause her crying for a second. She froze, focusing all her attention on the one thing that mattered. Listening.

Again, she heard it, although it was faint.

Was that . . . *a breath?*

Jumping back, she stared at the lifeless man. Her hand flew to his face, prying open one eyelid, then the other. His pupils tightened in weak dilation. She pried the ear tubes of the stethoscope wide from her neck and secured the eartips firmly in place. Holding her breath, she held the cold chestpiece to his heart as she strained to listen.

"I've got a heartbeat!" she shouted.

The staff scurried to check his vitals, repeating her steps. Disbelieving or not, the medical team moved with urgency. Every second counted.

The colonel ordered, "Oxygen. Now."

The team gathered around the body again, working in tandem. A tug-of-war to yank him back from death's cruel grip.

~

The air-conditioning of the colonel's private tent should have been a welcome relief after the day she'd had, considering it was Kathryn's fourth sixteen-hour shift in a row. Instead, she seethed with irritation, fixated on the difference between this cushy space and their battle-ready operating room. Exhausted and wallowing in her own dried sweat, she resisted the urge to brush at the sand and dust stubbornly sticking to the uncovered areas of her skin.

The colonel studied her before speaking. "You did good

today." Nice words from her commanding officer, Dr. Carter Reeves.

She nodded, hoping the *fuck you* shooting from her eyes was received loud and clear as she sneered at him. "But?"

"But I've requested a replacement. You're going home." After a minute, he added, "No amount of wishing I would fuck off is going to change that."

Oh, good. He got the memo.

Too pissed off to waste time arguing, she pulled in a deep breath. "When?"

He cleared his throat. "Sooner than I thought. There was already someone inbound with experience. He was en route to another assignment, but I managed to have him reassigned here."

"How convenient. So, tomorrow?"

"The day after," Carter said with a shrug. When she gave him a cutting glare, slicing a hole right through their wall of rank, he lost his temper. "Dammit, Kathryn. Give me a break. You lost it today."

Unable to control herself, she shouted, "Goddammit, Carter! I saved a life that everyone, including you, gave up on."

His volume matched hers as his palms hit his desk. "Look me in the eye and tell me you're raring to go for another day of losing one life after another."

Defeated, she swallowed her tears and dropped her heated gaze to her dusty combat boots.

"You can't keep this up," he said, softening his tone. "After my first tour, I'd had it, swore I'd never return. I had to come to grips with my own humanity. We all have our limits, and I can see in every torn-up piece of you that you've reached it and then some. Hate me all you want, but I've got to get you out of here . . . before you're shattered beyond repair."

He stepped closer. "Just because we're no longer married doesn't mean I stop caring about you, Kat."

"I hate it when you call me that." Annoyed, she stood, turning to head out.

"Hang on." He snatched a business card from his desk and handed it to her. "Look, we're all entitled to a break, and I know you're close to a decision on re-upping your Reserve status."

"Hey! Kicking me out of your unit is one thing, but if you even so much as think about screwing with my career—"

He grabbed her hand. "You know I'd never do that. I'm just saying . . ." He placed the card in her palm. "Explore your options."

Kathryn took the small piece of cardstock, curious as she read the print.

WOLFF INVESTIGATIONS
Z. Wolff – Senior Partner

The toll-free phone number and Denver address were embossed in raised ink. Unconsciously stroking a finger over the letters, she asked, "What the hell is this?"

"An opportunity. Zach's an old friend. He founded a company that looks into insurance fraud, and he asked me if I knew anyone with medical expertise I could recommend. He needs someone tough. Someone who won't give up until they get to the truth. And he's willing to wait for the right person, so you can think about it. You don't have to make a decision, but at least talk to the man. You need a break, Kat—" He stopped short, correcting himself. "Kathryn." His tone softened again. "Before *you* break."

She crushed the card to a wad in her fist and stormed out of Carter's tent. As she stomped across the compound, a few stubborn tears pushed from her eyes. "Goddammit."

Furious, she tossed the crumpled card to the ground. Then stopped. Whirling around, she bent over to retrieve it, and stuffed it deep inside her pocket, eager to shove down the inevitable.

Hugging herself tightly, Kathryn struggled to breathe. Everything was spinning out of control. Desperately, she looked up at the star-filled sky, oddly calmed by the strange evening serenity often lacking in the war-torn country.

Tormented, she sighed into the dry desert air, bracing herself for a gut-wrenching change.

CHAPTER 5

KATHRYN

Present day

The soft down comforter covered Kathryn's legs, but she was still cold. Unable to see, she found herself chilled even more at the sound of the door opening. Her rattled nerves squeezed shivers from her as she listened to each slightly muffled footstep approaching on the soft carpet.

Through little gaps where her cheeks met the blindfold, she caught a glimpse of a man's laid-back but stylish loafers beneath his jeans. Biting her lip, she pulled back a smile.

Damn, his shoes are big.

She flashed back to one rainy afternoon on a long college weekend when, for no reason other than idle curiosity, she dove headfirst into "research." A hop, skip, and mouse click later, she searched for studies on whether the size of a man's shoes said anything about his pocketful of potential.

Can't blame a girl for loving science.

One guy actually won a Nobel prize for his work, measuring stretched-out penises against other body parts.

Hmm, wonder which intern scored the coveted role of pole puller?

She imagined the announcement. *And in the category of Penile Possibilities, the Nobel prize goes to . . .*

The results of these studies? A correlation was negligible. Mr. Big Stuff standing before her might be her own hands-on experiment.

Still, staring down at the promise of his footwear, she barely managed to squelch a giggle or her growing blush. But her third-grade humor subsided as he remained standing there.

Quiet. Watching her.

His fingers were warm as they barely brushed across her hair, then dropped to scoop up her hand in a soft shake.

"Hello, Kathryn." His voice was low. Deep.

He squeezed her hand, and she shivered as she tried to hold in a shuddering breath. Then his hands moved to her shoulders.

"You're freezing. Let me turn up the heat, but . . ." He stepped out of her sliver of a view, then back, and she felt softness wrap around her arms and back. "Better?"

She tugged the robe, setting it higher on her shoulders. "Mm-hmm. Funny, I never thought you'd be *adding* clothes to the equation."

"Well," he said, his voice carrying from farther away, "this place costs a pretty penny. If we're smuggling a souvenir out for you, you'd better love it."

Laughing, she pulled the cozy plushness tighter and relaxed. "I absolutely do."

The momentary cheeriness subsided as he returned, pointing those shoes—and she could only imagine what else—straight at her. The heat of his body washed over her, and her breathing stuttered to a halt.

"Breathe," his gruff voice gently commanded, and she obeyed, sucking her lungs full of air before slowly easing it out through her lips. "Good."

The mattress lowered as he took a seat beside her, covering her hands in both of his. "Don't worry, Kat."

Her voice cracked slightly as she lied. "I—I'm not worried."

"Then why the frown?" He cupped her cheek for a second, then dropped his hand.

"I—I prefer Kathryn."

Did I really say that? To him? For once in my life, maybe I could break a rule or two, let someone else in on my nickname. I mean, it's practically for medical research. Hello? Shoe size.

"Well, *Kathryn*, we're not doing anything tonight—"

"Because I want you to call me Kathryn? Seems harsh." Regretting her back talk, she realized that sassiness might be an unwelcome trait in a sub.

His voice lowered. "Isn't that what you're here for? Something . . . harsh?" His finger traced up her spine with a hot, electric charge that dropped her head back, releasing a gasp from her lips. He tugged away her scrunchie, freeing her long hair and combing it out with his fingers.

She whispered, "Yes," followed by the immediate panic of, "No . . . I mean, I don't know. I'm sorry. I'm— "

"Relax," he said, massaging her neck and shoulders. "Like I was saying before I was so *rudely* interrupted . . ." His voice was low but playful. Hypnotic. Alluring. Making every last one of her defenses drop into the palm of his hands. "We won't be doing anything tonight. And no, not because you want me to use your go-by name."

He kissed her cheek, and the kinship was immediate. Only military or ex-military would use a term like *go-by name*.

"Never apologize for what you want. I insist on knowing your desires," he said softly, and she shivered as his breath tickled her ear. "I have wants too, *Kathryn*. I want my frisky little kitten not to worry too much about showing off her claws." His hands kneaded harder. "We're not doing anything because I heard you loud and clear. Your hard limit."

No sex? No way. Why the hell did I say no sex?

Don't listen to her. She's a crazy lady.

"I—"

"You called your hard limit, and I won't cross that boundary. At least, not tonight. I can't take advantage of you just yet. And certainly not until I see a smile back on those beautiful lips."

A shy grin emerged from her as his thumb brushed the fullness of her lower lip. Her mind tripped over one tawdry thought after the other, like sucking down that hot finger he'd been teasing her with.

"While you're cranking those gears in your head," he said, "let me make you an offer."

"An . . . offer?"

He stood and took her hands, lifting her to her feet. Seconds later, the rustling sounds captivating and concerning her were unmistakable. He was turning down the bed.

Anxious, she swallowed the ball of tension in her throat as he continued.

"Unless you object, I'm lying you down and covering you with the comforter to keep you warm. I'll be on the other side. On top of the covers."

What? "Why?"

"Because I need you comfortable. If you're relaxed, you'll be easier to get to know. I need to know what you're thinking so I can understand why you're here. And what you want."

She turned to ask him a question, not realizing he'd changed positions once again. The accidental smack of her hand hit his solid chest.

"Sorry," she said, panicked as she yanked it back.

He picked up her hand and held it to his chest. Doing nothing at all, really. Somehow, it made her calm.

She felt his heartbeat.

His breathing.

And nothing made her feel more at ease. Like . . . coming home.

"What if," she asked shyly, "I don't know what I want?"

He huffed out a laugh, whisking her into the cradle of his arms.

"Don't worry," he said, reassuring her as he laid her on the bed. He tucked her in, adding, "I ask terrific questions."

It was strange how a blindfold made her lose all track of time. And dropped her resistance.

For the first time in, oh, ever, she finally let it all out, yammering on and on for far longer than was socially acceptable. A firehose of TMI, she described her string of disappointing sexcapades, not worried for a second how it made her look.

I'm blindfolded. In a hotel room. Lying on the bed and divulging all my sexual experiences to a stranger with expertise in BDSM.

Let's call it therapy.

And all the while, her attentive, albeit anonymous "therapist" continued to listen.

"I feel like you're suffering," she said, "having to hear all this. Like a bad date where the girl can't stop talking about her exes. Unless, of course, you've fallen asleep."

On cue, a snore erupted, and without thinking, she swatted him. Nervous, she again tried to pull back, but stopped as he grabbed her hand and chuckled.

"You need to trust yourself. You feel like something's missing, because it is. It's that simple." He rolled closer. "You know when you're not satisfied, Kathryn."

His words were gruff, yet soft. Filled with understanding. And something about the way he said her name was like he knew her. Knew her like no one else.

Biting her lip, she pushed out a confession. "Well, on more than one occasion, I've been accused of being"—she sighed—"frigid."

He laughed low. "Don't believe the hype of self-centered assholes. And don't bite your lip. When you're with me, consider that my job." His hand cupped the back of her neck, but he didn't squeeze. His whispers warmed her ear. "Listen to your body right now. Your breathing. Your heartbeat. You know what you want."

Her head barely nodded as her nether regions lit up like the Fourth of July.

"You're not frigid, Kathryn. You're lost . . . desperate to stave off your own instincts." He shifted his weight, dropping his grasp and moving away from her as he lay back. "You're not the only one fighting demons. Mine have kept me away for a while."

"Away from what?" she asked.

"From this," he said.

Curiosity might kill the cat, but she couldn't help asking. "How long?" Impetuous or not, she'd thrown it out there.

"Three years," he said on a long breath.

Holy shit. "You haven't had sex in three years?" Blurting it out, she winced.

"No, little girl. I didn't escape from a monastery." He caressed her cheek, and she smiled. Then his touch was gone. "But I haven't been myself. I've been . . . lost. Given up a lot of old habits. And thought I'd left this life behind." His deep voice held a note of despondence.

Resolved to overstep whatever Dom/sub rules were in play, she clumsily stumbled out of the comforter. Kneeling toward his side of the bed, her blindfolded eyes staring presumably at him, she said, "I probably look ridiculous, but I have to face you when I ask you this. If you haven't been a Dom in three years, why are you doing this now?"

His tone smoldered through her. "Because, Kathryn Chase, in a strange way, I understand you. And in *this* world, you need to be looked after. I can do that. Keep you safe and protected. Let you play. And explore." His hand massaged her knee.

Her lips curled up. "Like a naughty guardian angel?"

"Naughty guardian? Yes. But you're the only angel here."

She lowered her head, with both her hands now playing with

his fingers. "What if I try something and don't like it?" She shivered again.

"You're cold. Lie down." Before she could shimmy back under the blanket, he said, "No. Next to me."

Uncertain, she felt her way forward, letting her hands travel to his chest. He pulled in a deep breath, and she got a solid feel of a man built for endurance.

Suddenly worried, she stopped.

His hands wrapped around her, pulling her close to him and nestling her body in his hold. His heat and strength were so strangely comforting, her tension evaporated.

"Listen to me carefully, kitten. You're here for my pleasure." He kissed her forehead. "And I'm here for yours. I'm not here to push you beyond what you can handle."

His fingers wove through the silky strands at the nape of her neck, then closed, latching on as he pulled her head back and made every molecule of her body tingle. His next words came out on her lips.

"My rush comes when you beg me to take you to your limit."

Please, she thought as her lips quivered. *Take me to my limit. At least point me in that direction.*

Leaving her unkissed, he released his hold and slid his hand down her back, where he rubbed gently. "Stay curled up if you like. Tonight, and only tonight, I'm on your terms. Even if it's just this." At her silence, he whispered, "But there's something else you want. Isn't there?"

Yes.

Tracing figure eights across the muscles of his chest, she whispered, "There is something I'd like to try."

CHAPTER 6

JAKE

Jake sent the text from the hallway outside the hotel suite, half enjoying the thought of interrupting Paco, who was likely in a private VIP room in the hotel spa. His smile grew as he imagined the man sipping a bright pink cosmo from a chilled martini glass, lounging back for a heavenly foot massage until he snapped up at the chime of Jake's text.

This should get him up here in under a minute.

JAKE: *She needs you.*

He checked his watch and waited, his smile growing. *In three, two, o—*

Ding.

When the elevator opened, Jake beamed. "Right on time."

Paco's eyes narrowed with concern as he stalked over. "What happened?"

"Nothing. She's fine. But she's been behind that blindfold for all this time. I didn't want her taking it off alone."

Paco leaned against the wall, his arms crossed, stating the

obvious with a hint of mischief. "There's no reason you couldn't stay. Help her take it off."

Jake chuckled. "Funny, she said the same thing. But I'll promise you what I promised her. Next time. If she wants to. But I want her to think it over before deciding. I slipped my number in her purse and told her she could call me. Anytime."

∽

Kathryn sat on the side of the bed, as if she hadn't moved in hours. She heard footsteps. Excited, she smiled.

He's back.

"Would you like me to do the honors?" Paco's cheerfulness was bathed in tenderness.

Disappointed, she shook her head and tugged the soft eye mask over her head, then dropped it to her lap. The silky fabric held her aimless stare as her fingers traced the edge.

He took a knee before her, coaxing her gaze. "Everything all right?" he asked, his subtle accent sweetening his sincerity.

She shrugged, pulling in a shuddering breath before meeting his eyes. After a minute, three words slipped through her shy smile.

"I want more."

CHAPTER 7

JAKE

As he strolled out of the hotel, Jake let his thoughts drift, the feel of Kathryn's skin still fresh in his mind.

Not to mention the sting. And the rush.

Deep down, he knew. Returning to the cage he'd just burst free from was impossible. She was his muse, and he'd be her maker. It was more than a feeling—this was an undeniable connection drawing him back to the land of the living.

She'd been with who knew how many men—*well, not that many*—but none could give her what she needed. As if her body existed only for him, in every way his touch demanded.

Far from cold, or timid, or even shy, she'd had a white-hot flame within her, raw and ready to be unleashed.

Or leashed. Whichever.

He thought about it.

A leash? Handcuffs? What would she like?

His pulse spiked. He had to know Kathryn's wants. Her needs. She'd be too easy to spoil. With a woman like her, he needed to pace himself. She had enough experience to know what she didn't like, but was practically a virgin in every way that counted.

Still, he'd been away from this life for so long. He wasn't

about to take things too quickly. Her body was begging to be his new journey . . . a feast of slow, salacious satisfaction.

As if in a trance, he returned to his truck. He'd never recall how. Yet he could easily rattle off every dirty little item he'd scrolled through on his cell as his ass stayed planted in the driver's seat in the parking lot.

With Kathryn still in the hotel, he wasn't going anywhere.

Perusing the spicier sex paraphernalia passed the time while he waited. He had to. There was no way in hell he'd leave without knowing she was safely on her way.

She'd clung to him until their last tender kiss. Tearing away from her lips was its own sadistic form of torture, because he sure as hell didn't want to.

I had to. She named her hard limit.

I'm not breaking her trust. No sex.

He thought it over.

Seriously, no sex? What the hell was she thinking?

Frustrated, he sat. His cell phone perusals were building the tension in his pants. The more he clicked and shipped this toy and that to fill his empty treasure trove, the more he was tempted to take his aching matters into his own hands.

But he couldn't. He needed to focus enough to look up every minute or so to make sure he didn't miss seeing her leave.

If he knew Paco, and he'd like to think over the past few years they'd gotten as close as people in covert circles tended to get, he could gauge Kathryn's frame of mind by Paco's overprotective parenting.

If Paco was worried, he'd drive her home.

Less worried, and he'd walk her to the car.

Not worried at all and at her insistence, he'd let her walk out by herself.

A moment later, out she came. On her own.

Jake smiled as she strolled to her car, looking as fresh and sweet as he'd left her. Between the imaginative array of kinky candy filling his online cart, and watching her soft curves, pale flesh, and perfect strawberry-blonde hair spilling down her back, his bulge demanded some air.

He undid his jeans.

He couldn't wait to see her again.

If she calls.

Of course she will.

The wad of cash she'd tried to pass him said that much.

It was ridiculous. And adorable.

He chuckled at the sight of a fellow guardian keeping a watchful eye out. Paco inconspicuously spied on her from a nearby window. A text popped up on his phone.

PACO: I see you too.
JAKE: You know me. Trust-but-verify kind of guy. Just making sure she's good to go.

Do I ask or not?
The suspense is killing me.
What did she say?

He waited for the bouncing bubbles to finish on the text.

PACO: She showed me your note.

Between his below-the-waist discomfort and Paco's cool coyness, Jake finally texted his aggravated need-to-know in one word.

JAKE: And???

He looked back up, and Paco was gone.

Son of a bitch. That's my move.

JAKE: Fine. I'm both glad and perturbed at your ability to be a vault. So, fuck you. Thank you. And safe flight.

Three emojis were texted back . . .
A martini glass.
A plane departing.
And the little round winking guy blowing a kiss.

CHAPTER 8

KATHRYN

Stunned and thoroughly seduced, Kathryn hugged the far right lane as she drove home, barely breaking the speed limit. Her hijacked thoughts swayed back and forth to the tantalizing temptations of the past hour.

It dawned on her there was little evidence of their encounter. The bottle of water she was still nursing. The ghost of his touch on her body. And a note he'd slipped in her purse. The little square had the hotel logo at the top, with his phone number scribbled across it and two little words:

KITTEN TAMER

I think he means kitten trainer.

The bashful smile previously pasted on her face widened.

His low, dark, raspy commands echoed in her thoughts. Under his spell, she'd obeyed.

Willingly.

Easily.

Without hesitation.

On all fours, she'd crawled across his lap and waited, painfully patient as her willpower yielded and her pleasure bloomed. All from him. His power. His control. His touch. Enslaved by his unconditional hold on her hot and bothered hoo-ha, and all without actual, bona-fide sex.

Her pussy was putty in his hands.

He seriously needs those babies insured, she thought as her mind drifted back to their time together . . .

∼

He'd started slow—agonizingly slow—skating one lazy finger in a sensual trail up the back of her thigh. That same sexy finger she'd wanted to swallow whole. The way he worked it teased her with a taste of things to come, sending her straight past the cobwebs of a rarely tapped corner of her mind prominently labeled DOWNRIGHT DIRTY.

He'd insisted she stay still while he worked. The sweet torture forced her hands to fist the comforter. Her breaths became choppy, erratic. On the verge of losing all control, she squirmed, aching for more of him. He had total control, and she handed it to him, a man who knew how to take that power and bend it to satisfy her deepest yearnings.

He could be anyone. Is that turning me on?

Her uncontrollable whimpers grew louder.

Definitely a turn-on.

Feathering her skirt hem across her skin, he'd lifted it up, finally resting it across her back, exposing her butt. The cool air against her hot skin had been a relief, pushing a sigh from her throat. Her panting had become so heavy and fast, she felt dizzy and dropped her head.

"Breathe," he commanded in his deep voice.

No sooner had her inhale released than she felt the sting of his hand.

He'd slapped her ass.

Hard.

Her cry sliced across the room, so loud and unexpected, she'd tried holding it back. But the next smack drew out a throaty scream from her. It subsided as his hand rested across the fleshiest part of her ass, holding her skin . . . then caressing it before sliding across to the other cheek.

His other hand had wrapped around her throat, softly stroking her after each slap. His thumb brushed across the fullness of her bottom lip.

"More, kitten?" he'd asked, his voice raspy.

What he asked hadn't been a real question. Or rhetorical. He'd said it more as if they both knew. She'd been thirsting to death on a desert island, and her body wanted to plunge into the deep end of this clear blue pool.

"Please," she'd begged before sucking the thumb he'd pressed into her mouth.

As he delivered fierce smacks across her other cheek, her moaning sounded as if his thumb were covered in decadent dark chocolate.

Ready, she arched her back to receive another smack, and he'd dropped it so swiftly, a shudder cascaded from her dizzy head to her curling toes.

Much too soon, he pulled his thumb from her mouth and draped her skirt back over her stinging buttocks. Her head dropped as she struggled to keep herself up on all fours.

Without warning, he'd moved her to her back on the bed. Before she could ask, she'd been covered by the blanket again. With a tender kiss, it was over.

Half-panicked, she'd asked, "Did I do something wrong?"

"No," he'd insisted, taking her hand and brushing his hot lips against her fingers. "You're perfect. And I'm human. It's time to stop. You have all you need to think things over."

With another kiss, both her breath and his deflated at the bittersweet judgment call.

∼

How she'd gotten home, Kathryn couldn't say, but before she knew it, her car pulled into the garage at the back of her condo. Killing the engine, she did out of habit. Aimlessly sitting there was out of necessity. Preoccupied, she continued in a weak attempt to process it all.

The lurid spanking session had left her . . . addicted.

He's right. A BDSM dime bag was just the taste I needed to think things through.

She resigned herself to the only conclusion. *I'm a sub.*

And he was a god, a nameless, faceless stranger who lifted her sky high by commanding her to her knees. She'd give anything to feel the smack of his big, hot palm against her needy backside again.

What's a good cooling-off period before I call?

He said call or text anytime.

Is that an hour? A day? More than a day?

Do I ask about his day?

Is this "dating"?

Tearing herself from the eternal treadmill of wandering thoughts, she finally got out of the car with a mental note to text Paco in the morning. Maybe there were books she could read, something like *Ground Rules for Doms and subs*, or *Delving into BDSM for Dummies*.

Deep in her thoughts, she walked on autopilot into the condo. Without thinking, she entered the dark but familiar hallway, dropping her purse and keys on the counter. She kicked off the mistake of a shoe buy and relaxed her feet on the cool tile of the floor.

My notebook. All her interviews had pages of chicken scratch and doodles, until she transferred her notes to her laptop. The six-by-nine, dollar-store notebook had at least two hours' worth of work waiting for her.

But it was safely tucked away in the pocket of the driver's-side door of her car. And her feet were insistently steered in the direction of the bathroom.

It can definitely wait. There's no way I'm tackling work tonight. First things first.

She needed a shower, if for no other reason than to tango with the detachable showerhead and finish the job started by her ringmaster. Stepping farther inside, she flipped on the lights.

Then froze.

Her home was a disaster. Sofa cushions and pillows were scattered across the floor. Every drawer of her desk had been pulled out and flipped upside down. A disaster zone that could only mean one thing.

I've been robbed.

Distressed, she whirled around to grab the phone from her purse. A moment later, she felt it. For the second time that night, someone landed a blow on her body, but this time to her skull, knocking her to the floor.

Curled up and clutching her head, she slumped on the tile, overcome by confusion for a few seconds before she was swallowed by darkness.

CHAPTER 9

KATHRYN

"We'll do our best to find the assailant," Detective Scott Delaney said, reassuring her.

Kathryn admired his salt-and-pepper hair, trimmed high and tight around his ears. *Military cut.* "You a vet?"

He nodded, a smile replacing his stoic expression. "Navy back in the day. You?"

"Army." Grinning, she exchanged a glance of unspoken competitiveness with him. "Well, since you're helping me catch the scumbag who blindsided me, I'll hold off on giving you too much crap for the poor decisions of your youth."

He chuckled. "Hey, I'm proud of every one of my questionable choices, and have the tattoos to prove it. Say what you will, but the Navy always gave me assignments with an ocean view."

"You got me beat there. And envious. I never got a chance to see the ocean, though I flew over several back and forth to the desert." Her expression fell as she steadied herself in a short stride to the freezer. An ice pack would quiet the persistent throbbing of her head.

"You all right?" he asked. "I can call a paramedic."

"I'm fine. Just need to reduce the swelling," she said as he helped her to the sofa.

"Well, looks like they got in through an unlocked window off the balcony. Seems to be a lot of trouble for a standard break-in. Once you do an inventory, let us know what's missing. But you said nothing's gone from your purse?"

She nodded, keeping the cold gel pack on the pounding knot at the back of her head. "Most of it. All my credit cards and cash are still there, but I usually keep a few business cards handy. They're gone. Or, at least I thought I still had a few in there. And my laptop is missing. It was on my desk."

The detective motioned to the forensics team, showing them where to dust for prints. "The chances of us getting your computer back is a long shot."

She dropped the ice pack and raised her head. "I'm not worried about it. Nothing's on it. It's a shell. Everything is uploaded to a virtual desktop in the cloud. My company will just issue me another one, and all my information will be magically available as soon as I log in. Basically, they got away with a fancy four-pound paperweight. I've got more technology in my phone than on that system."

"Well, you probably scared them off before they took more." Delicately, he touched her shoulder. "You sure I can't take you to a doctor?"

She nodded with a weak smile. "I'm okay. I used to be a nurse. No impact to my vision. No slurring of speech. I know the date. Bush is still president, right?"

Delaney's kind grin did a piss-poor job of concealing his concern.

She laughed, waving off his worry. "I'll just have a nice goose egg for a few days. Nothing a little good old-fashioned aspirin or two can't cure."

"Are you comfortable staying here tonight?"

Disappointed, she looked around at the work ahead of her. It would take more than a few minutes to get everything back in place. *First thing tomorrow.*

"I'll hunker down. Looks like they got everything they came for. And if they wanted to hurt me more than they did, I'd be on the eleven o'clock news. Besides, several neighbors saw your festive red lights and have offered to help with whatever I need."

Delaney pulled out his card and handed it to her. "Here. My direct cell's on it. Call me anytime, day or night."

Noticing the bright gold band on his ring finger, she asked, "Doesn't your wife mind when random strangers call you at all hours?"

"Nah. She's a lawyer with the DA's office in Colorado Springs. She knows the drill, and the reason I'm here. Your company's a long-time consultant to them. I guess your boss is worried." When Kathryn gave him a defiant teenage eye-roll, he said, "Let me do one more check to secure all your windows, and then we'll head out."

She rubbed an especially stiff knot in her neck. "Thank you," she said, grateful but ready for some peace and quiet.

After all the drama of a bizarre, stressful day, she bypassed the shower after Delaney and his team left and spent half an hour soaking in the tub. With her cabernet long gone and the delicate weight of slumber tugging at her eyelids, she got out. Her skin was a nice pink, holding the heat of the water.

Curious, she glanced in the mirror, twisting to get a better view of the slap marks on her butt. Her eyes gleamed as she admired the red hue of her new friend's handprints burning across it.

She measured her own hand against the outline.

Well, if foot size and butt stamps are any indication, this guy will be a hell of a lot more than a handful.

CHAPTER 10

KATHRYN

*E*arly the next morning, Kathryn tackled the catastrophe of a crime scene. Coffee in hand, she put everything away bit by bit, hiding all evidence of the botched break-in. Looking around, she couldn't shake it. Something felt wrong.

Her gaze lingered on the desk that seemed bare without her laptop. She knew the insurable value of it far exceeded the street value, which would be $200, tops.

Her puzzled gaze swept back and forth across the room. If the culprit's loot was limited to an inexpensive laptop and a few business cards, something was off. She bit her lip, grabbing her purse to reinspect it. In order to grab the business cards, they'd have to ignore the credit cards and the stack of twenties neatly tucked in her wallet.

"At least they left my souvenir." She pulled the kitten-tamer note to her chest, then slipped it back behind the twenties.

It was a lot of cash to carry around, especially for Kathryn. In her defense, she hadn't planned to return home with it. Not wanting to be rude or make assumptions, she'd made a hasty stop at the ATM before meeting Paco that night. He'd assured her all expenses were covered, but she wasn't sure if that included all his friend's... services.

Innocently, she'd asked her mystery man if a situation like this required a tip. He'd refused with a charmed laugh, caressing her cheek and taking nothing more than one last kiss. "Good night, Kathryn," was all he said before heading out.

She licked her lips, his taste still fresh in her mind. Her fingers brushed her lower lip, then pressed against her temples to relieve her head. The intrusive throbbing was getting worse. Another couple of aspirin would be great, but would have to wait for whoever was knocking at her door.

The delivery man handed her a box that was the perfect size for a new laptop, but couldn't be—it was way too light. It required a signature, and she recognized the return address as Excelsior/Centurion, a long-term client of Wolff Investigations.

Intrigued, she closed the door and lightly shook the box, hearing only the slightest rustle.

After tearing open the box, she laughed out loud. Delighted, she pulled out the Four Seasons bathrobe and hugged the plush, pristine terrycloth. Swinging the slice of heaven around her, she could almost forget the headache nagging for attention. But *almost* wasn't good enough.

At least they didn't steal my coffee.

After downing a couple of generic pain relievers, she took her coffee with her to the balcony to wait for the meds to kick in. A gust of brisk air hit her as she stepped outside. She swaddled herself tighter in the plush bathrobe and tugged the collar to her nose, breathing in memories of the night before. As she took a seat in her all-year wicker patio lounger, the chill swept away her grogginess. Her alertness and focus returned.

Methodically, she studied the balcony.

It presented one hell of a jump to access, as it hung one-and-a-half stories over the garage. From every angle, she couldn't figure out how anyone could know that the balcony's sliding door was unlocked. The nighttime below-freezing lows kept all her windows shut.

Lucky guess?

Even so, rolling the dice in the hopes it would be unlocked was a crazy gamble for a burglar.

And why?

There were a dozen other condos in her building, practically gift wrapped as easy marks. She peered over the railing. Two condos down, one neighbor opted for the carefree Colorado life, hardly ever bothering to close their garage door. It remained open around the clock.

Plus, the back alleyway always had someone coming and going, leaving their home or returning to it. A parked car might not have drawn suspicion, per se, but would have fired up a busybody or two on the condo association. Hell, half of her immediate neighbors were on the board. Nothing filled their lives like hanging out with family, potlucks, and waving the hundred-page association rule book in a neighbor's face.

Friendly reminders, my ass.

So, the perpetrator or perpetrators had to have walked, which would be inconvenient for a hasty escape. And piled on the risk.

Kathryn thought for a second. *This wasn't a random or impulsive act. It was specific. Deliberate. And targeted.*

On me.

A sudden dizzy spell forced her to ease back into the chair and close her eyes. Petting the expensive plush sleeves covering her arms, she quietly mumbled to herself, "They went to an awful lot of trouble. They're looking for something, maybe related to a case. If I had my laptop—"

A series of loud knocks at her front door snapped her from her thoughts.

Perfect timing.

Slowly, she stood, careful at first. Confident she could pick up the pace, she quickened her steps.

The knocking broke through again.

"Coming," she shouted. The computer would require her signature, and a delivery person would only wait so long.

She gazed through the peephole, pleasantly surprised to see the man holding the package. Opening the door wide, she said, "Detective Delaney. Moonlighting with Best Buy?" She smiled as he handed the plain brown box to her. "Come in."

"Thanks." He entered as she tore open the cardboard and worked her way through the Styrofoam padding to unwrap the computer and power cord. "I went ahead and signed for it."

Amused, she teased him. "Wow, they let just anyone sign."

"Almost anyone. This helps." He grinned as he flashed his badge. "And Tony delivers for us too. Listen, we seem to have a break in your case."

She plugged in the laptop, pausing when she spotted his frown. "Then why do you sound less than thrilled?"

He scratched his head, and a strange uncertainty transformed to a low scowl. "One of the fingerprints turned up in our database. I'm not sure how to say this . . . but I know the guy. Well. Really well. He's a volunteer emergency medical technician—"

"An EMT?"

Delaney nodded. "I've worked with him for years. Not that any of that would make an impact on the case. It's just . . ."

Hesitation shadowed his expression, and that bothered her.

The laptop forgotten for the moment, Kathryn made herself comfortable on the sofa while the detective took his choice of comfy chairs. "It's just what?"

Wringing his hands, he shook his head. "He says he's innocent."

"Standard answer," she said, knowing the detective probably heard that on a regular basis.

"And he needs to see *you* to prove it."

Her eyes widened. "That's different. He wants to convince me?"

Shrugging, Delaney continued. "Look, I'm going out on a limb here—big time—but if there's a chance he didn't do it, I'd hate to keep him locked up. And, to the great disappointment of my wife, I'd bet my house he's innocent. But he won't talk to me, and he's always talked to me. He says it has to be you."

Contemplating the bizarre request, she looked away.

"I know how it sounds. And all I've got is a hunch. How about this?" Delaney said. "I can drive you to the precinct, and you can check him out from behind a two-way mirror, then decide if you want to speak with him or not. Nobody will tell him you're there. And if you do decide to speak with him, I can accompany you. Afterward, no matter how it goes, I'll bring you back."

Kathryn couldn't put her finger on why, but she trusted Detective Delaney's judgment.

Nursing had taught her the finer points of peeling back onions. Symptoms were never the biggest threat—the underlying cause was. It took discipline, diligence, skill, and sometimes a little something most people chalked up to as *luck*. But she thought of it as something else.

After three years of investigating insurance fraud, she'd honed her skills even more. When it came to working a case, she trusted her intuition.

Sniffing out the truth became her superpower, like a bloodhound catching whiff of prime rib. But sometimes, at the end of the day, she'd be left with a shit-ton of nothing more than her gut feelings, and trusting her instincts always paid off.

She looked at Detective Delaney. Here sat a man betting the bank on a hunch because he'd been right case after case. And at the end of the day, a gut feeling was good enough for her.

"No," she said, "I can drive myself and meet you there. The last thing I want to do is incarcerate an innocent man. And I'm as curious as you are as to why he'd want to see me."

Through the glass of the two-way mirror, the man handcuffed to the hard, steel table was, well . . .

Gorgeous.

In worn-in jeans and a black T-shirt that molded across him too perfectly for words, he sat. Patiently waiting, casually almost, as if he were on a park bench enjoying the day. His impressive good looks and the tousled waves of his hair gave him an easygoing air. Natural.

"Wow," she said softly.

"What?" Delaney gave her a curious look, and the quick small shake of her head satisfied him.

She couldn't see the entire tattoo peeking out from beneath the man's sleeve, but its significance was clear. *Memorial ink.* A silent tribute to fallen soldiers close to one's heart.

"Do you know him?" Delaney asked.

Turning, she met the hopeful eyes of a detective who looked like he'd gone weeks without sleep. She turned her attention back to the man awaiting her verdict. "I'm not sure. I need another minute."

Her stall tactic was just a ruse. She had nothing. But taking her time was deliberate, and she didn't want to make a hasty decision. After all, he might need to leave here for his underwear shoot with Calvin Klein. The public outcry would be too much. She had to be sure.

But at this angle, he didn't look familiar. She'd interviewed dozens of people for several ongoing cases. Maybe he was one of them.

After a few minutes, her staring started to feel invasive. Here was a man worried about going to jail, and all she did was ogle him. About to shake her head in defeat, she paused when something on his neck caught her eye.

The scar was long and smooth. Far from a run-of-the-mill flesh wound, it streaked up across the muscle of his neck.

As if he could feel the heat of her stare, the man rubbed it.

From its closeness to the jugular vein, whatever had injured him had come way too close for comfort. Evidence that something had been within an inch of taking this man's life.

Needing to be sure, she nearly knocked her head into the glass as she stared harder.

I know that scar.

It came from a bullet . . .

And me.

Scars are a snapshot in time, but don't always come from just one source. This one might have been born of a rogue bullet but was sealed by medical stitching, and she'd been his seamstress.

Closing her eyes, she remembered her patient's body, certain that this man's shirt concealed four more wounds scattered across his torso. Badges of bravery branded on his skin from his last-ditch attempt to save others . . . and a lifelong testament to what he'd survived.

He turned toward the mirror. Startled, she grabbed her mouth, failing to hold back a gasp.

"Yes," she said slowly. "I know him." Turning to the detective, she asked, "Can I speak with him?"

Delaney's eyes widened, but he nodded. "Yeah. I'll be watching you from here. He's secure; just stay on your side of the table." He nodded toward the door. "Through there."

The interrogation room was clean and uncluttered, but cold with hard lines and a bleak gray tone. A little intimidated, she stayed near the door. As it shut, she spoke slowly.

"I know you, don't I?"

The man nodded, half standing in an odd gentlemanly manner for someone shackled to a table. She took the metal chair opposite him. When she pulled it out, the legs screeched against the floor.

Cringing, she planted her butt quickly on it, then blurted out, "Next time, I'll ask for wheeled chairs."

"Leather and reclining, if you're taking requests," he said.

She swallowed, trying to peel her gaze from him.

God, you're good looking. Please be innocent, she thought, then reconsidered. *Okay, "innocent" isn't exactly the right word.*

"Your neck." She pointed to below his left ear, and he tilted his head to give her a better look. "You got that scar during a mission where you nearly died. Or technically, *did* die before you were resuscitated. You're Sergeant First Class Russo, aren't you?"

He nodded again. "Jake," he said, inviting her to a more casual conversation.

Choked up, she reined in her tears. "I can't believe I'm seeing you in the flesh. Right in front of me. You look . . . amazing."

As she relaxed, wiping her eyes and now laughing at her own forward comment, he chuckled.

"I mean, oh . . . you know what I mean. The last time I saw you, you—" She stopped herself, swallowing her grim words. Relieved, she smiled. "And here you are. Good as new. Better, even."

Without thinking, she leaned closer and her hands nearly touched his, but froze at a tapping on the glass. Kathryn turned, catching a glimpse of herself and Jake in the mirror, and she yanked her hands back.

Clearing her throat, she asked, "But why did you break into my place? If you need money—"

Jake sighed out a laugh, giving her a good look at his mesmerizing hazel eyes. "I'm good on cash, but I appreciate the gesture. And I didn't break into your place. I have an alibi."

"But they have your fingerprints," she said, her worry bleeding through.

He nodded, conceding the unfortunate discovery. "Yes. Yes, they do. And there's a reason."

Jake clasped his cuffed hands, and she waited.

Whatever he was struggling to say was taking forever. With a gentle voice, she spoke. "Look, I promise we can work it out. I won't press charges, and I'll make sure my company doesn't. I'd really like to help. If you'll let me."

"Kathryn..."

His voice sent a shiver through her. She couldn't escape whatever was happening between them. His eyes seemed darker than a second ago.

God, what I wouldn't do for you, she thought, just as he spoke again.

"You're my alibi."

Okay, I might draw the line at lying to the cops.

"Me?" She leaned toward him. "Hey, I really . . . *really* want to help you out, but," she whispered closer, "I can't tell them that. Even if I wanted to cover for you, I wasn't anywhere near here. Before I got to my apartment, I was halfway across town in a public place. People saw me . . . alone."

Well, at least that's what people saw.

"Maybe you'll think it's less of a leap when I tell you where I was." He steepled his fingers straight at her, and with a squint and a smirk, he repeated her words. "Halfway across town . . . public place . . . people saw me."

Confused, she stared at him. The echo of her own words wasn't exactly helping.

He finally said softly, "Taming a kitten."

Her squinted eyes flew open wide. "Oh my God," she blurted, jumping to her feet.

She darted to the mirror, giving it a few swift knocks.

"He's innocent. It wasn't him. I can vouch for him. I—" She turned to Jake, her face scorching from the roaring heat of an unforgiving blush. "I'm so sorry. I—oh my God, and I—and you—"

She spun around as Detective Delaney entered the room.

Once the cuffs were removed, Jake rubbed his wrists. He towered over her with a meaningful stare that held her still. She dropped her gaze, desperate not to die right there on the spot of suffocating embarrassment.

Delaney shook Jake's hand. "Well, glad this all worked out. But I didn't catch everything you said. What's the alibi?" The detective's inquisitive glance bounced between the two.

Kathryn jumped in. "He was on a . . . uh . . . blind date. *He* was the blind date. That I'd set up. Through a friend."

"With you?" Delaney squinted, confused.

Jake broke in. "With a remarkable woman. Someone Kathryn knows very, very well."

Kathryn topped his convenient truth with a dollop of cold, hard facts. "And it wouldn't have been over in time for him to do anything at my place, because he was in Denver when it was all happening."

She nodded enthusiastically, coaxing Jake to nod along. He did, with a gleeful glance back at her.

Delaney pushed further. "And the fingerprints?"

Kathryn's fumbling for words caused Jake to break in.

"Were they on her purse? When I met my *date*, I found that purse lying out in the open. I moved it for safekeeping until she could break away from whatever was holding her back." He shook his head with a chuckle. "Girls who don't secure their belongings are just begging to be punished."

Jake threw his muscular arm around Kathryn. Her gasp was quiet as he tugged her body close.

Delaney looked at Jake in disbelief. "I'm sorry. I don't believe this at all."

"Which part?" Kathryn asked before sucking in a guilty breath. Her exhale escaped with the tiniest whimper as Jake's fingers skimmed the small of her back.

The detective laughed as he peered at Jake. "Did you just say *you* were on a *date*?"

"I was," Jake said with a grin so wide, she dropped her face to the palm of her hand. "Because of this one right here. On one hell of a blind date with an unbelievable woman who knew exactly what she wanted."

The detective landed a few hearty pats on Jake's shoulder. "Well, good for you. I'm glad you're finally getting back into the dating scene. What's she like?"

Kathryn's ears perked up.

"Oh, you know the type," Jake drawled, and her eyes widened. "Gorgeous. Smart. With a fiery side that draws me in."

His warm hand slid lower, falling perfectly across the handprint hidden beneath her jeans.

Her yelp flew out before she could stop it, forcing her to bolt from his touch. "Well, glad I could help."

She raced out the door, down the hall, and out the precinct doors, ignoring the cries of "Kathryn, wait up!" coming from behind her. Relieved that her up-front parking facilitated her escape, she jumped into her car and started it with trembling fingers.

As she sped away, her heart pounded, and her mind descended in a tailspin of disgrace, desire, and pure debauchery.

She'd torn away from him. From that big, brawny, ripped, lickable *him*.

Maybe I've earned myself a spanking...
Stop it! Get a grip.
Yeah, I'd love to get a grip...
Oh my God, I sound like a sex maniac.

Her visceral tug-of-war between angel/devil mind dominance was understandable. Or so she rationalized.

For years, Kathryn had been haunted by the body of Sergeant Russo. The last she'd seen, he was stable but lifeless. Bloody. Bruised. Helpless, and nearly hopeless.

But holy shitballs, look at him now. Apparently, one taste of death turned this man into a smoldering rock-hard body perfect for sex and sin.

It was him. Last night. My mystery Dom.

Seducing out my secrets. Teasing with that finger that wouldn't quit. Touching. Spanking. Taming.

The two men who'd brought more of her raw emotions to the surface were one and the same. Dealing with it all was a challenge. She couldn't process everything she was feeling, though the wetness weeping from her core was a hell of a clue.

Desperate to relieve her spiking body heat, Kathryn pressed hard on the button in the door, somehow willing the window to lower faster. Blazing a trail home at seventy miles per hour, she barely felt the icy blast of the thirty-degree breeze.

What the hell is that man doing to me?

CHAPTER 11

JAKE

"Kathryn!" Jake ran after her, not giving a damn how loud he was in an echoing hall of a police station. Had his phone, wallet, and keys not still been locked up, he'd have been in the hottest pursuit of his life.

He called out one last time, pounding his determined feet down to the front doors. Watching her car speed away into the distance, he blew out an amused huff. Captivated, he smiled as he watched until her car vanished.

I'm not through with you yet, little kitten.

After grabbing his belongings from the front desk, he ordered a Lyft home. Delaney offered him a ride, but the last thing he wanted was to keep the conversation going with Scott. He'd rather pass the time figuring out how to get closer to a certain sub-on-the-run.

He didn't have Kathryn's number, and the likelihood of her calling him after an escape like that? Powerball had better odds.

Determined, he pulled out his phone during the ride home and checked in with his failsafe source for tracking people down. The all-knowing Facebook.

Bingo. There she was, in a myriad of snapshots that balanced campy and goofy with kind and sincere. A natural beauty who rarely wore more than mascara and lip gloss, she shared the warmest parts of her life across the internet.

No drama. Just a constant string of happy times with family and friends. And a fairly regular night out with the girls on Thursday nights at a local bar.

Lucky me.

After passing through the iron gates of his property, the Lyft meandered up the long driveway. For the first time in a long time, Jake felt it. He was coming home.

No, not the lavish cabin hidden on a heavily wooded hilltop. Despite the multimillion-dollar price tag, it was just his residence. Home was somewhere deeper, buried inside him below the heavy burden of guilt. Until last night, he hadn't been sure he'd be capable of balancing his wants and needs against his raw, uncut emotions. To trust his own mind.

Four friends lost. *And nearly a fifth.* His split-second reaction nearly cost him one of his own.

Disgusted with himself, it took him a good year of rebuilding himself from the inside out before he could face his own reflection in the mirror. But with Kathryn, he felt different. Connected. She was just the catalyst he needed to reset his mind. Focus on his wants. Let himself feel alive again.

But first things first.

After paying the driver and going inside, he hit the shower. Washing away the few hours of time in a jail cell was priority number one.

Not that he was a stranger to lockup. An adrenaline addict with anger management issues tended to enjoy the regular bar brawl. But that made waking up behind bars just another Saturday morning. And he was respectable now.

Semi-respectable.

His hands caught his eye. They were unscathed, which was a new twist after lockup. He supposed his self-imposed house arrest contributed to that—his own version of home confinement with one boring day followed by the next. At least he could keep up appearances of being a man in control.

Strike that. A Dom in control.

Half the time, he embraced his life as a well-adjusted and contributing member of society. *In control.*

And the rest of the time, he was bored out of his fucking mind. He could feel himself on edge. Dangerous. *Losing control.*

His current work was deep in the internet, chasing criminals and nefarious masterminds around cyberspace, catching bad guys and protecting his employer. In theory, not hugely different from his former life. But a world of difference in reality.

He was the good guy. The hero. Crushing the criminal underpinnings across the world wide web with a few lines of code, like a souped-up video game that he was damn good at winning. But it wasn't the front lines.

This new life was comfortable.

Very comfortable.

Dull-as-fuck comfortable.

Rubbing his hands together, he calmed. His body demanded a high-octane battle fix, and fighting was his release. Matched with an angry drunk equal in brute strength usually did the trick. Jake wasn't in it to pound someone senseless. But nothing suppressed his unsettled mind like feeling the pain. It let him breathe.

Still, the stale stench of jail gets old. Fast. And his dark tendencies seemed to take a back seat when he found a better way to fight his demons. He tore a page out of Nurse Chase's playbook and became a volunteer emergency medical technician.

Medicine was love at first fight. Uncooperative patients were his spirit animal. Never knowing what he'd be walking into filled the void of needing the unexpected. Over the last couple of years, he'd honed his skills, balancing the right mix of physical strength, compassion, and a laser focus on what *they* needed—his patients.

They might be a druggie on his third OD. Or a stroke victim. Maybe an active shooter who'd been taken down.

And then there were the children. Those were the best days, and the worst. But he'd be their gentle giant, treating and protecting them, if only for the moment.

No two days were alike, and Jake liked that, because he could work his shifts around his regular job with irregular hours. It became his relief valve. And nearly two years of one emergency after another bestowed him with a supreme gift...

Perspective.

He understood the ungodly circumstances Kathryn must have battled day in and day out—losing one life, and then saving another. An EMT, like an ER nurse, would never get to know the people they'd impacted most. It was just another day. Another joy. Another unspeakable anguish.

And she'd wrestled through both emotional journeys with him.

~

For the next few hours, Jake caught up on work, half laughing, half dreading the phone call from his boss.

"Jail? Again?" Mark asked. "At least tell me it's something exciting ... like, you've been charged with prostituting yourself? No judgment. At least you're getting out."

Jake chuckled along with him. "Um, no. Through a bizarre set of circumstances, I happened to be the lead suspect in a B-and-E investigation." As silence set in, Jake cringed, knowing Mark was patiently waiting for him to elaborate. "Let me start by stating I didn't do it."

"That's the guiltiest thing you've ever said. What did they have on you?"

"Fingerprints."

"Fingerprints," Mark said slowly, like an epiphany would hit him at any moment. "And what were your fingerprints on?"

Jake swallowed, then cleared his throat. "A, um, purse."

"Uh-huh." Mark didn't even try to hide his amusement. "Let me go out on a limb and assume it wasn't *your* purse. Do I have to ask, or are you going to tell me?"

Jake quickly fumbled out his explanation. "Look, you know me. I'm not into petty theft, and we're not working on anything that would need hands-on investigating. It's . . . personal."

"Personal?" Mark chuckled, obviously having way too much fun with this. "I'm glad to know there is such a thing as that with you."

"Fine," Jake said on a long exhale. "It's Kathryn Chase."

"Oh." Mark took a minute, then added, "That's interesting." His tone wasn't nearly as jovial as a second ago.

Concerned, Jake asked, "Interesting, how?"

"Well, let's just say your paths were about to cross anyway. For other than *personal* reasons. Remember Zach?"

"Wolff? Yeah. Wolff Investigations."

"That's the one. He's got a case, and I'm intrigued enough to bring in the big guns. You and the team. And out of my own pocket."

"If it's on your dime, I guess the sky's the limit."

"As if you need a bigger headquarters. But yes, the sky's the limit. Don't cheap out. The guys deserve better than that crappy instant coffee you had last time."

Amused, Jake huffed. "Fine. One state-of-the-art coffeemaker coming up. I'll probably need a new truck to haul it in with too. Maybe an additional room to properly store my new barista wear." He chuckled, and then his jabs at the boss stopped. "But what does this have to do with Kathryn?"

Mark answered, but only after a low growl exploded in a shout. "Goddammit," he barked. "I'm about to lose big-time, and all because Alex and Paco were fucking right. I can't keep my big mouth shut." He blew out a breath. "Ms. Chase is Zach's lead investigator on the case."

No fucking way. Was this the case Paco mentioned was coming my way?

To be sure, Jake asked his boss, "What did you say?"

"You heard me. Go ahead and give him a call so you can get caught up. I've got a bet to square."

"I will," Jake said, regretting how eager he sounded.

"Oh, I know you will. And have fun," Mark said cheerfully, ending the call.

Jake smiled. *Oh, I intend to.*

Before springing himself on the elusive Ms. Chase, Jake had a few things to check off his to-do list. Digging a little deeper into the break-in at her place was first on his list.

With a few keystrokes, he bypassed the PD's firewalls to sneak a peek at the police report. *Dead end.* Only the basic information was available. The full report hadn't been uploaded yet.

That's not like Scott. He's probably double-checking that I'm not in it. But the little that was there was enough to send Jake past mildly concerned straight to protective.

He checked the time. Kathryn's weekly meet-up with the girls for drinks was less than an hour away, something her Facebook time stamps had clued him in on. Making his way to the walk-in closet, he ran a palm over his scruff, uncertain about the right outfit for bodyguard duty.

After flipping through his closet twice, he found the task was tougher than he'd thought. Suits weren't his style, and the venue would be crowded and casual. Besides, once a girl's seen you in your everyday wardrobe at an interrogation room, pretty much anything's a step up.

She might not even show, he thought, then reconsidered. *She'll be there. After today, that girl needs three things . . .*

Besties.

Booze.

And maybe a little after-party binding.

His thoughts wandered back to every part of Kathryn's beautifully bent-over body. Her creamy skin glowed under the stunning brightness of a blush that just became his new favorite color.

His hand ached to smack that gorgeous ass pink again, but he wrapped his grip around his cock instead, containing his throbbing need. Eventually, he decided on a pair of loose jeans, a good call to withstand whatever might *come up*, then decided on a basic white button-down shirt.

His imaginative mind reeled with one dirty thought after another, and his pants choice seemed to be agreeing with the bulge of his concealed weapon.

Jake smiled. Being this close to Kathryn Chase was like a taste of chocolate after a three-year sugar hiatus. The rush was exhilarating.

His mind, like his pants, was pushing his limits.

I might need another shower.

What the hell is this woman doing to me?

CHAPTER 12

KATHRYN

"Sorry I'm late," Kathryn blurted to her friends when she arrived at the restaurant.

The foursome had met in nursing school years ago, and immediately bonded over a love of appetizers and their shared lifelong need to help others. Nothing beats a tough day better than a free-for-all vent session during half-priced happy hour.

As Kathryn plopped into the empty seat at the table, Dana and Laurie were elbow-deep in devouring their wings, while Julian was pushing around some scraps of lettuce on his plate, with the audacity to call it dinner.

Kathryn glared at him, grumbling. "Seriously, you're giving me a complex. When are you going to eat something?"

"When you show up on time," he said, pointing his fork at her. "If that day ever comes, I'll eat a whole damn pizza in one sitting. Now sit your ass down, take a load off, and tell us what the hell happened. You were robbed?"

Laurie waved for the server, who promptly delivered the pre-ordered vodka tonic for Kathryn.

With more wings on the way, she let it all out. *Nearly all.*

Okay, none of the really juicy details, but everything related to the robbery.

"Do you need a place to stay?" Laurie asked, handing over the basket of wings to share until the new order arrived.

Kathryn grabbed one and tore into it, shaking her head. "No, but thank you. I just can't figure out what they were after," she said, waving her chicken wing in the air as she muddled through her thoughts. "Or why they'd go to what seems to be a heck of a lot of trouble for hardly anything. But I promise you, I'll get to the bottom of it."

When she noticed the worry on her friends' faces, Kathryn raised a hand. "I'm fine," she said, but when Dana reached out to caress the back of Kathryn's head, she winced. "Ow."

Dana gave her a scolding look. "Fine, huh?"

The second basket, still steaming, was set before them.

Famished, Kathryn grabbed a fresh wing. "Nothing that a few more wings and a little of this heavenly tonic can't cure. Cheers."

She lifted her glass, and the others reached in to clink theirs.

"And the cherry on the hot fudge sundae is that since this afternoon, I've been getting a string of random calls from skittish guys, heavy breathers, and the grossest, most bizarre men. I couldn't keep up with blocking them all. I had to shut off my phone."

Smirking, Julian fixed his gaze over Kathryn's shoulder. "Speaking of gross, bizarre men."

"Drinks are on me," a familiar and unwelcome voice said from behind her.

Kathryn slumped when she heard the voice. Turning to him, she forced a smile. "That's sweet, Artie. It really is. But we're good."

"Hey, if you're trying to save me money, no need to worry. I've got plenty of it." He leaned so close to her ear, the moisture of his whisper made her skin crawl. "Besides, I thought you liked a take-charge guy. That's what your ad said, right?"

Adrenaline shot through Kathryn, and she jumped to her feet and shoved the man out of earshot of her friends.

"Careful," he said, scowling as he brushed at his chest. "The last thing I need is a stain on my brand-new shirt." With his best seductive look—which captured all the charm of a man fully constipated—he arched a brow. "It's Armani."

Unamused, she planted her hands on her hips. "What are you talking about?"

"Giorgio Armani?"

With a swat to his arm, she huffed. "Not the goddamn shirt, Art. What ad?"

"Craigslist, baby. I mean, your name wasn't on it, but I'd know those digits anywhere." Grinning, he traced her shoulder with a finger.

Furious, she narrowed her eyes. "If your paw isn't off me in one second, I'm ripping that finger off and shoving it up your ass."

The initial fear in his eyes morphed to confusion. "Wait, did you want to be a Dominatrix? Not that I'm complaining. I must have misread the ad."

He pulled out his phone and swiped at the screen. Finding the ad, he started reading it aloud before she snatched it from his hands.

No. This can't be happening.

She'd placed the ad weeks ago, thinking that if worse came to worst, she was just going for it. And there would be plenty of time to cancel it if she changed her mind.

How could I forget to cancel the stupid ad?

Returning his cell, she put on her sternest, most serious game face. "Look, I'm only going to say this once. This ad might have my number, but it was an obvious mistake."

In more ways than one.

"You're a super-sweet guy, Artie. Our date was nice."

And your tongue down my throat was just what I needed to keep you out of my condo, no matter how rich you are or how much you needed to pee.

"So," she said as sweetly as she could manage, "I'm going to return to my friends, and you're going to find a great girl worthy of your growing collection of restaurant franchises and miniature horses."

"They're quarter horses," he called out to her back as she quickly returned to her table.

"He's absolutely smitten. And super rich." Laurie pointed out the facts with a suggestive song in her voice as Kathryn sat back down.

"Not rich enough," she said flatly. "We went on one date weeks ago, and you'd think we were getting engaged. At least with my phone shut off, all the nutso romantic memes have stopped. Glass half full, I guess."

Closing her eyes for a second, she realized the memes would now probably be taking a turn for the worse.

Desperate to shake off the vibe of the day, she took a quick swallow of her drink and let out an appreciative moan. Famished, she tore into the scrumptious bits of barbecue chicken, relaxing a bit after finishing one wing and then reaching for another. She glanced up to find Julian staring.

"Hey," she said after quickly swallowing her mouthful. "No judging. I'm stress-starved, and I've had a long day."

Julian's smile spread wider. "Oh, honey. Trust me, you're always in a judgment-free zone. I'm just a little jealous. I've been making eyes at a hot guy at the bar, but it's clear he hasn't been able to take his eyes off you since you came in." When the ladies all turned, he whisper-shouted, "No! Don't all turn at once. Dana and Laurie can casually take turns."

"What about me?" Kathryn asked, with her back to the bar, and Dana handed her a mirror from her purse.

"Oh my God," Laurie whispered. "If you pass, I definitely call dibs."

"No way," Julian said quickly. "I saw him first, and I definitely get a crack at that piñata." He waggled his brows as he slid a martini olive off its spear with his teeth, following it with a tiger growl and a seductive chomp.

Kathryn held up the mirror. Jake's face reflected back at her as he lifted his beer bottle at her in a toast. She swallowed and whirled around, as if this tiny mirror had totally hoodwinked her. Seeing him here in all his unbelievably hot glory brought on a rather loud gasp.

Like a dirty little deer stuck in the headlights, she froze, uncertain what to do. From across the room, he raised one brow as he mouthed the word *breathe*.

Without thinking, she blew out a breath.

He cracked a smile and hopped off his stool. As it was the only vacant seat at the bar, he patted it, offering it to her. Freaked out, she turned to her friends.

"Oh, son of a bitch. He's totally into you," Julian said with a pouty scowl.

"Well, maybe if you'd eat a wing every now and then," Kathryn said to him, then asked the girls, "How do I look?"

Dana was already reaching out with a wet towelette to wipe down Kathryn's face while Laurie cleaned up her hands like she was a toddler. Fresh as a baby's bottom, Kathryn chugged down her drink and headed over to the bar.

Battling the inconvenience of a small dizzy spell, she focused on him as the music seemed to tick up louder. Climbing her butt on the stool was a little clumsy. Her sheepish grin erupted into a giggle as Jake grabbed her around the waist and deposited her onto the seat.

He leaned close to scold her quietly. "I can't believe you ran away."

Worried, she frowned, but he smiled.

"Running away and frowning at me in one night," he said. "I might need to punish you right here and now."

She giggled again, then sobered. *Wait. Why am I giggling at that?*

With a teasing expression, he leaned in. "Your friends missed a spot."

Mortified, she reached for a cocktail napkin and swiped at her mouth, but he said, "I'll get it."

With an appreciative nod, she handed him the napkin, but he took it and tossed it aside. Cupping her face, he grazed her lower lip with the ball of his thumb. Instantly, her lips parted as her eyes fell shut.

"I've almost got it," he said softly, then pressed his mouth to hers, slipping his tongue through. She suckled it with a loud moan.

At least the blaring music is drowning out my sex sounds. And what's with me sucking whatever he sticks in my mouth?

Another moan carried her through the heavenly kiss. He pulled away, stroking her cheeks until her heavy lids lifted. "Barbecue?" he asked with a smirk, and she nodded.

"Yup."

They both laughed, though Kathryn's died down with another wave of dizziness.

"Are you hot in here, or is it just me?" Puzzled, she looked at him, and his smile widened at her flattery. "No, I mean the room. Is it hot?"

"I'll get you some water." Jake signaled the bartender and ordered a glass of ice water.

Stealing the opportunity, Kathryn looked back at her friends.

Dana and Laurie were all kinds of thumbs-up and fanning themselves. Julian had his phone held high, obviously filming. Kathryn swatted at them and turned her attention back to the hunk holding the glass.

"Here."

She took the cold drink and sipped, but instantly set it down with a flash of nausea. Her focus was cloudy. "The music is so loud."

"You look a little flushed. I can't imagine why," Jake said, joking. "Let's get you some fresh air."

Her weak nod invited him to help her off the stool, but when she slid off, she fell heavy into his arms.

"Kathryn?"

She couldn't answer. Her knees gave out and she collapsed with the faintest echo of his voice in her ear.

"Stay with me, kitten."

CHAPTER 13

KATHRYN

As Kathryn came to, she concentrated, trying to shake off the grogginess. Bits and pieces of hushed discussions dragged her eyes open. The dim light of the room made her struggle to pull everything into focus as she tried sitting up.

"Easy." Dana gripped Kathryn's shoulders, holding her on the leather sofa.

She was in an office, surrounded by her three best friends. Fortunately, her besties represented some of the finest medical professionals in the city.

"Do you remember what happened?" Dana asked.

"Oh . . ." Kathryn moaned with regret, flinging her forearm over her face. "I'm afraid I do."

Julian tapped her arm. "You know the drill, sister. Let's go down the list together. Is there any chance—"

She waved her hand for him to stop. "I could be pregnant? I know, I know."

A husky voice came from behind her friends huddled around her. "Perhaps I should step outside."

Kathryn pushed Julian out of the way to see Jake heading out the door. "No, don't go. I'm not pregnant." She smacked Julian's leg. "I'm probably a little dehydrated, with the altitude and all."

"Or this guy's kisses cause women to faint." Dana turned her head to Jake. "I can only imagine what other superpowers you might be harboring."

Laurie looked down at Kathryn. "Or it might have been that blow to the head."

Jake stepped closer and his gaze locked on hers. "What blow to the head?"

Is he . . . worried?

Laurie told him everything she knew. "She was robbed. Some lowlife douchebag clubbed her good for a laptop and some business cards. What the hell is this world coming to?"

Jake nudged Kathryn's friends aside and sat next to her, gently working his hands over the back of her head. She flinched, but braved the soreness by biting her tongue, preventing any more moaning at his hands.

He lifted her chin, studying her eyes. "A knot like that . . . and fainting. Could be a concussion. Looks like I'm taking you to the hospital."

"Oh no. That's okay. Dana, or Laurie, or Julian can drive me."

All three objected at once, each giving different reasons for not touching their friend in need with a ten-foot pole.

Jake's crazy adorable eyebrows and mild smirk coaxed out Kathryn's grin. She looked back at her friends, who were busy making an imaginative range of silent lewd gestures behind his back.

She sighed at Jake. "Well, sounds like I'm stranded."

"Lucky me. I'll be your driver."

CHAPTER 14

KATHRYN

Despite the connections Kathryn and Jake both had at one of Colorado's finest emergency room, it still took a while to prep her for imaging, capture the shots, and get a clean bill of health from the radiologist on duty. She rested a little easier to learn there was nothing of concern, and was relieved to be released.

Cradled in the upscale leather seat of his F-150 Raptor as he drove her to get her car, she glanced around the kickass truck, which provided a conversation starter. "So, Jake . . . what do you do?"

Worst post-hanky-spanky line ever.

"Isn't it obvious?" he said, and she shook her head. "Guess."

Unsure, she shrugged. "Construction?"

"Computer science," he shot back with a ring of pride in his voice.

She nodded slowly, trying to make peace with the polar extremes of his personality, and he reached over to squeeze her knee.

"Hey, not all geeks drive Teslas."

His hand stayed on her leg, preventing its uncontrollable bounce as she tried to carry on the conversation.

"How'd you get into that?" she asked.

She knew bits and pieces about Jake. Pretty much whatever she could learn after she'd returned to the States. He'd been part of a covert team. An action guy. So, her nervous question could be taken as natural curiosity.

His jaw clenched as he pulled his truck into the parking lot of the bar. He yanked his hand off her knee, frowning as he slowed his truck to a stop without a word.

"Sorry, I didn't mean to pry." She reached for the door handle, but was stopped by his strong grip on her wrist.

His eyes remained focused on the sight straight ahead. "Stay here."

With a flip, his high beams flooded her car in light. Kathryn and Jake stared at the lone car remaining in the parking lot, a Honda HR-V. As far as she could tell, everything seemed fine.

Jake reached over her to pop open the glove box and pulled out a Colt .45 ACP.

Okay, things aren't fine. And that's the biggest gun I've ever seen.

The handgun looked enormous compared to the 9 mm pistols Kathryn was used to handling. She only possessed a weapon when it was issued to her, whenever she ventured to dangerous assignments overseas.

His thumb flipped the safety. With a stern expression, he unlocked his cell and handed it to her. "Call Scott Delaney. And lock the doors behind me." He waited for her acknowledging nod before getting out.

Worried, she quickly scrolled through his contacts, getting the detective on the phone and filling him in while she watched Jake check out the car. She couldn't see whatever it was that alarmed him.

"He's just walking around the car," she said, feeling helpless as she watched. Her nerves hit a new high as he pointed the weapon at her car. The driver's side. Then he slipped the barrel through the slightly ajar door and opened it wide.

All this fuss because I forgot to shut the door? I was in a hurry. And hungry. He must think I'm scatterbrained, irresponsible . . .

Or begging for a punishment.

Blushing, Kathryn decided she needed a dose of cool air, and hated keeping the detective waiting. About to open the door, she unlocked it just as Jake headed back. He climbed in and took the phone.

"Scott, you're gonna need forensics. We'll wait until you get here, but Kathryn's still recovering from that blow to the head. She looks . . . flushed."

Jake's grin sweetened as his eyes locked on her. "I really need to get her home . . . Yes, she is. And she needs some rest . . . Okay, see you in a few."

After disconnecting the call, Jake turned to her. "He's in the area. He'll be here soon."

She nodded, feeling squeamish to ask why he seemed to be on high alert. Obviously, this wasn't all because of a door left open. "What did you see?"

He huffed out a slow breath. "I'll tell you, but not yet. How about we pass the time by you telling me what you've been up to. Specifically, what you've been working on?"

Her knee began another round of bouncing. "I'm an investigator. Insurance fraud. I . . . really can't tell you much more than that." She swallowed hard, apologetic in her defiance.

"So, you haven't told anyone about the cases you're currently working on? Not even your closest friends?"

"Never. It's critical that I lay low. Otherwise, trails start vanishing and evidence disappears." She shifted in the firm leather seat, angling her body to better face him. "But there is one I had to call around about. Maybe I spooked someone. Or—"

Blaring sirens closed in. The strobing red lights of two cars swept across the parking lot, then shut off.

FALLEN

As Jake opened his door, she grabbed his arm. "Your turn."

His gaze darted to her hand around his bicep, and then to her eyes.

She pulled her hand back, certain she'd committed some major sub faux pas. *Maybe I needed to ask permission first.* Embarrassed, she crossed her arms tightly across her chest.

His eyes lightened at her response, and he slipped his hands in to unknot her arms. "Kathryn—"

"Don't worry. It's fine. I understand. I overstepped my bounds."

"What?" His hands cradled her jaw. "No, it's not that at all. I'm not your Dom here. I'm just . . ." His long exhale delayed what he was trying to get to. "Just protective. It's disturbing. The scene. I hate what I'm about to ask, but I think you should look at it. With your training, you might catch something."

He stroked her hand with his thumb as she watched the team surround the car.

"You think I'd catch something the cops wouldn't?"

Shrugging, he said, "It's, um, a hunch."

She nodded. "Can you at least let me know what to expect?"

"Someone left one of your business cards on your front seat," he said, and she waited, knowing the other shoe was about to drop. "With a knife stabbed through it."

She sucked in a breath and tore from his grasp, scrambling from the truck and storming past the forensics team to the driver's side of her car. The quiet, timid kitten just became an enraged mountain lion. Furious, she had to see the damage for herself. As she took in the scene, Jake's hand slipped through hers.

"I understand it's upsetting."

"You bet your ass it's upsetting," she shouted. "The son of a bitch sliced my brand-new custom-leather seat. This car is only a few weeks old. Motherfuc—"

"Kathryn," Jake said calmly. "This is a new car, so it locks automatically when the key fob is out of range. Where were the spare keys?"

She blanked, and blindly stared back. "They were in my desk drawer, but now that I'm thinking of it, I didn't see them when I checked for anything missing." Her eyes fell shut. "Dammit, he has my keys."

"It might be a she," Delaney said, interrupting as he stepped up to join them.

Confident, she shook her head. "Not a chance. The only reason women cut up any part of a car is out of jealousy, and trust me, the stab wounds wouldn't stop at one. And I haven't been with a guy in . . ."

Jake stepped forward, crossing his arms with a smug grin.

"Anyway, the point is, odds are we're dealing with a man." She peered at the seat. "That's my business card, all right, and," she leaned in closer, "that's one of my kitchen knives. But . . ."

Trepidation set in as she squinted, studying the scene harder without disturbing the evidence. Her expression fell as the reality of what she was looking at dawned on her.

Jake's hands squeezed her shoulders, his warmth sinking in. "What is it?"

Her breath shuddered, spurring him to rub up and down her arms. Nothing about it was sensual, just caring. In an instant, all his tenderness brought out her emotions. Determined, she fought every impulse to fall back and take comfort in the arms of a man she barely knew, yet someone she had way too many feelings for.

She shrugged him off, determined to stand on her own two feet, and glanced at the detective. "Can I see your pen?"

Delaney handed it over. She made sure the ball point was retracted to avoid any marks, and slowly outlined the area where the cardstock surrounded the knife.

"See that rim of caramel coloring? Right where the knife meets the paper?"

"Yes," Delaney said, nodding.

She struggled to calm herself, though her pounding heartbeat was doing its damnedest to shut down her ability to speak. "I know where it came from. I had an apple just before my shower . . . before I met my friends here at the bar. I took a knife from the butcher block and cut the apple into slices, then set the knife in the sink. When I came back to the kitchen, I saw a box of Ziploc bags out, but I'd been tidying up so much, I figured I just missed them." She looked at the men. "That's my knife, and the guy grabbed it while I was showering."

"He might have grabbed it much later," Delaney said calmly.

Sadly, he was wrong.

"He used the Ziploc to carry the knife. It prevented fingerprints. But it also kept the juice from the apple from drying, which would have happened pretty fast with how dry Colorado is. That's the discoloration—the caramel stain where the knife meets the card. Simply put, it's oxidized apple juice. You need to go back and dust my place for prints again. There might be new ones."

Jake took her hand firmly, not giving her the option of letting go. "And you need a safe place to stay. He doesn't just have your spare car keys, Kathryn. He has a set to your condo as well. I know somewhere you can stay, and it's more secure than Fort Knox. State-of-the-art security system. Limited entry."

Her weak head shake was instantly halted by his hand cradling her cheek.

"I insist."

Exhausted, irritated, and on the brink of a major breakdown, she gave in with barely a nod. "Can we drop by my place for an overnight bag?"

Delaney held up a hand. "The two of you aren't going alone. I'll have an officer meet you there. We'll check it out first, and you can go in while we dust for prints again."

Jake wrapped his arm firmly around her, only releasing her to help her into his truck.

∼

With Jake on her heels, Kathryn stepped in her front door and shivered, noting that her cozy condo had turned strangely cold.

Unfamiliar.

Frightening.

The kitchen was just as she'd left it, except for the missing knife now firmly planted in her car seat. But her gaze fixed on the counter. The empty counter. Where the box of Ziplocs had been.

Could the creep have left and come back to retrieve them? *Not a chance in hell.* The asshole had been there the whole time. She had to have been within a foot or two of bumping into him in her own hallway earlier.

Kathryn retraced her steps, her solid resolve slowly crumbling as she realized she hadn't closed the bathroom door fully when she showered. Her arms tightened across her chest, holding in her shiver. Shoving down her fear to keep her tough-as-nails facade took a lot more than a few deep breaths.

Pull it together. The bastard is messing with your head.

Jake entered the kitchen, but she slipped past him, avoiding his eyes at all costs.

"I'll just need a few minutes to pack."

His hand swiped across her arm, but she ignored it.

Weeping, she tugged her sleeve to her eyes, losing the war against those stubborn tears. Her thoughts were way too preoccupied to focus on what to take. For all she knew, she'd shoved eighteen pairs of panties in her bag, and not one top or pair of pants. But it didn't matter. The bag was packed, and her head was killing her. So, with her overnight bag in one hand and her pounding head in the other, she slowly stepped out of her bedroom.

The bastard got my keys, just to fuck with me. What else did he do?

Wandering through her condo, she scanned room after room,

and stopped at her new laptop. Her finger skated along the top, tracing several circles on the surface as she thought. Blowing out a breath, she dropped her bag to grab some aspirin.

"Something wrong?" Jake asked.

"He didn't take it this time." Filling a glass with tap water, she popped the pills, then continued. "I'm guessing he knows he can't do anything with it without my access codes. I don't trust it."

"You've got amazing instincts. I'm living proof," Jake said with half a grin that she couldn't help but return. He tapped the computer. "How about I take a look?"

"No, don't worry about it. I'll just have my company send me another one to wherever it is I'll end up."

"I'm happy to check it out."

Without waiting for her approval, he tugged the power cord free from the wall, looping it around his hand, and tucked the laptop under his arm.

Her smile of amusement said it all. Her head hurt too much to fake her skepticism. "Look, that's very sweet of you, but—"

Grinning, he extended his hand, taking hers for a shake. "Oh, I'm sorry. We haven't been properly introduced. Jake Russo. Veteran. Truck lover. Whiskey drinker. And lead cyber investigator for global technology corporation Excelsior/Centurion."

CHAPTER 15

KATHRYN

The ride to the safe house was quiet. Some might call it eerie. Seeing the gated entry, Kathryn couldn't help but wonder if she'd entered some sort of unmarked federal compound. The kind you only read about in books.

Thick woods darkened the winding driveway beyond the nearly pitch-black night. The high beams that had cast a bright hue on her car earlier did little as they rounded one dark curve after another up the hill. By his speed and relaxed steering, it was clear Jake could navigate the twists and turns with his eyes closed.

The driveway ended at a large contemporary building with straight lines and hard angles, giving the structure a foreboding presence. The standout feature contributing to the *don't fuck with me* atmosphere was that there were no windows on the first story.

The truck pulled into what for most houses would be the garage. Here, it opened to a huge bay sparsely filled with a few other vehicles, including a Range Rover and several motorcycles. Jake killed the engine and they both got out, the thud of their closing doors echoing against the walls.

"So, how many people are at this safe house?" she asked.

Kathryn's tired attempt to grab her overnight bag from the back was met by his hand swooping in. He threw a *you know better* scowl her way and slung the bag's strap over his shoulder before he showed her inside.

"Including you and me? Let me think." He mulled it over, counting on his fingers, looking to the ceiling as if it could help him through a complicated math problem. "Carry the one . . . oh," he said as he gave her a sly look, "that would be two."

Her smile slipped past her heavy fatigue. He was trying to lay a rosy red carpet over the swamp of crap she was wading through, and it was adorable.

Opening the door, he let her into a vestibule. Instantly, soft lights popped on as they made their way through a long corridor.

Motion activated.

They approached an ominous steel door. Jake pressed his hand onto a panel next to it. The loud clank snapped her from her weariness, letting her know the door had unlocked.

High-tech security too.

Well, even if my room is the corner suite at Alcatraz, I just need some sleep. Pretty sure it's got running water and electricity, so it'll be paradise compared to some of the hellholes I've bunked in.

Jake pushed open the heavy door to let her through.

Stunned, she reconsidered every preconception she'd had. Apparently, walking through the hall of MI-6 led them straight to the lobby of the Ritz Carlton.

The vaulted ceiling soared a full three stories above them, with a massive rustic stone mantel towering between walls of floor-to-ceiling windows. For a second, she could lose herself in the twinkling lights of the distant city and forget the whole reason she was here.

"This safe house is nicer than Buckingham Palace," she said. "After they catch the SOB messing with me, I just might stick around. Maybe I could water the plants or cook to earn my keep."

Her soft laugh earned her a slight chuckle from Jake in reply.

"Anything's possible. I've got an in with the owner. Here, I'll show you the room you'll be calling home for a while."

A half-spiral staircase took them to the landing on the second floor. Down the hall, he opened the double doors to a corner bedroom with a king-size poster bed and two walls of windows overlooking the same breathtaking view.

Jake ushered her inside the room and set down her bag. "I'll be right back. I'm going to grab you a few bottles of water. Do you need anything else? Snacks?" When she shook her head, he said, "Be right back."

Snooping around, she peeked into another doorway. The biggest bathtub she'd ever seen barely took up much of the spacious bathroom. A fireplace shared the wall between the two rooms.

Definitely going on my must-do list. Bath with a roaring fire.

The large walk-in closet was empty except for a few quilted blankets stored high on the top shelf, and she took another glance around. With the cream sheers and plush corner chair accented with a NAMAST'AY IN BED pillow, the room was lavish, but comfortable and cozy. A small photo in a silver frame on the nightstand tied it all together with a homey touch.

She picked it up, surprised to see a family photo depicting a much younger version of the man she'd spent the last few hours with. A candid shot, it captured an up-close-and-personal view of a young man graduating from high school, flanked by his beaming parents. For whatever reason, the sight of it brought tears to her eyes.

Convincing herself the response was perfectly normal for someone recently faced with extreme events and exhaustion, she didn't try to hold back the tears that slid down her cheeks.

When Jake's returning footsteps neared, she turned away, swiping her face and using her sleeve to dry the frame where a few drops had landed.

She cleared her throat as he stepped inside the room. "Looks like you're here a lot. I guess rescuing damsels in distress is just another day for a lead cyber investigator, slash EMT, slash knight in shining armor." She set down the frame. "Anyway, I'd hate to take a room you're used to."

He slung his arm around her shoulders as he gazed at the picture holding her attention. "I was eighteen, about to head off to boot camp and my first deployment."

She stepped out of his hold and grabbed the bag at her feet, not bothering to get too comfortable. "You take the room. Seriously, I'm really low maintenance. I'm happy to take a smaller room . . . or the couch. I'm just grateful for a safe place to sleep."

He stepped in front of her, tucking her hair behind her ear, and she dropped her bag. She looked down, foolishly trying to mask her crying.

Her breath hitched, but she said softly, "Or a tent out back . . ."

He lifted her chin, and her eyes fell closed. The press of his lips touching hers unknotted every muscle in her body. As he pulled her to his chest, she relaxed, unable to push away his warmth.

This man's too much for me. I barely know him.

But she was his. All his. At the weakest, most vulnerable point in her life.

He pulled back from the kiss, leaving her wanting.

"This is my home, Kathryn. And you're more than welcome to it. This is the room my folks stay in when they visit, but if you'd rather have a different one, there are several to choose from. If you need anything at all, I'm at the other end of the hall." He pecked her sweetly. "Feel free to mosey anywhere you want, but try to get some rest."

She studied his eyes, biting her lower lip. "Do you always come on this strong?"

Carefully, he slid his fingers to the back of her neck. His low voice sparked a shiver. "No, little kitten. Never in my life."

With the firmness of his grip, her head fell back. For the first time, she realized what she'd been too preoccupied to see.

He knew who I was. All along.

Becoming her Dom hadn't been a coincidence. Jake had chosen her.

She smoothed her hands across the muscles of his torso and slid them around him. His lips brushed her ear, and her nails skated over his back.

"And for the record," he murmured, "I've barely skimmed the surface of coming on strong with you."

The heat of his low voice vibrated against her neck, and she let out a little whimper.

His hand dropped to cup her cheek as he laid a last kiss on her lips. "Try to get some rest."

He headed out, closing the door behind him.

Once she had her pajamas on and having spent the last of her energy on unpacking, Kathryn welcomed the surrender of sleep. But not before looking at the photo one last time. Smiling, she pressed a kiss to her finger, carrying it to the young man in the frame.

CHAPTER 16

KATHRYN

Sleeping late had never been Kathryn's thing, but it felt good to rest. Jake barely bothered her at all as she slumbered until noon, occasionally bringing her food and checking in on her. He was so solicitous, the opposite of what she thought a Dom was supposed to be, it made her wonder if he really was one.

Later in the afternoon, he gave her a tour of the grounds. His property seemed to go on forever. When they returned to the house, he offered to run any errands she needed, but she declined.

Jake had been the consummate gentlemanly host. And she'd been way too comfortable as his guest. Shocking herself, she unapologetically crashed early, not long after dinner. Apparently, being stalked and attacked exhausted a person.

The second morning, Kathryn took charge as her early bird brain woke her with the sun. She figured she'd make good with earning her keep, intending to fix them both some breakfast with whatever she could find.

Slinking down the stairs with ninja-like moves in her flannel pajamas, she halted at the entrance to the kitchen and her tiptoed feet fell flat. The alluring aroma of dark, rich coffee hit her like a good-morning smack on the ass.

Sunlight bounced off the shiny surfaces of the gourmet cappuccino machine on the counter, teasing her with a come-hither gleam. Skimming her fingers across it, she murmured, "As if you had to ask. Good morning, you steaming-hot sex machine."

"Morning." Jake stepped in from the breakfast nook.

A flush warmed her cheeks. Trying not to gawk was too hard this early in the morning. *Damn, he knows how to wear a T-shirt.*

"Can I fix you a cup?" he asked.

Eager to show off one of her best skills, she smiled wide. "Oh, not a chance. I worked my way through my first year of college at Starbucks. This baby's all mine." Like coming home, she started prepping a drink, then noticed the mug in his hand. "What are you having?"

"Oh no, you don't. Yours first. I'll watch and see if I can pick up pointers from a seasoned barista."

She turned from his charm. Diving into a sweet cappuccino was just the wonderful wakeup she needed.

I could do this blindfolded.

Sneaking a glance at his scruffy mountain-of-muscle glory, she bit her lip through a silent giggle.

"Can I have some cream?" she asked, but he didn't respond. She caught his naughty grin and shook her head. "What am I going to do with you?"

His muscular body closed in. "Nothing," he said a little too directly, and set his coffee mug down, scooting the creamer across the counter toward her.

Her smile vanished.

I guess he's not a morning person.

Fumbling about, she finally managed to steam the cream to a thickness that allowed layering it into a leaf over the coffee in her mug. At least she could have a pretty cup of coffee with her first-rate faux pas.

Still facing the machine, she took a taste, but her body began overheating from more than the steaming-hot java. His fingers brushed her hair over her shoulder, letting his words whisper across her neck.

"Wrong question, little kitten. What you really want to know is what am I going to do with you."

His body touched hers. Well, a very specific and rigid part of his body did. Nearly spilling her coffee, she set it down.

Peering over her shoulder, he admired her artistry. "Impressive. How long will it stay like that?"

"Um, a few minutes."

She leaned back, sinking into the heat of being blissfully between her coffee and a hard place. His body cloaked hers. His hands tightened around her wrists, keeping hers locked at her sides. Like a wound-up jack-in-the-box, his kiss on her neck popped her butt to his groin.

His low voice rumbled in her ear. "How are you feeling?"

How am I feeling?

Like surrendering to that cannon of a cock giving me the stickup.

She tried to reach back, twisting her wrists to grab more of him, but it was no use. They were hopelessly shackled in his grip.

"Answer the question." His stern voice feathered the words on her skin.

Her head dropped back to his shoulder. "Oh, I think I'm perfectly fine for . . . whatever you have in mind."

His teeth tugged her ear. "Then we'll wait. Until you're sure." He released her and stepped back. "Turn around."

She did as he demanded, panting through her stillness. As his darkening gaze drifted down her body, she tried to remain still.

"We need a safe word," he said. "What would you like?"

I thought we weren't doing anything. Not that I'm complaining.
Her parted lips quivered. "R-r-red?"
"I like red."

He crossed his arms, stretching his cotton sleeves tightly around his biceps, and she sighed.

"You can use that, at any time, for any reason. I'll never think less of you for using it, but it'll be a total deal breaker if you need to use it and don't." His eyes lost their dark haze—their luster—leaving the emptiness of someone hollow. "Not a mood breaker. A deal breaker. Got it?"

She swallowed hard. "Yes."

"Good." His eyes reignited, alive with her understanding. "Now," he said as he leaned back against the counter, "take off your clothes. I'm dying to see you. All of you. Afterward, you can head up to shower while I fix breakfast."

His lips curled up as he finished the last of his coffee, watching and waiting.

Well, I can't very well let the man die . . . again.

Her teeth tugged at her full lower lip, not really reining in an ecstatic smile. The wanting gaze of those gorgeous eyes tore through whatever inhibitions she might have had.

"Turn around," he said. "Slide off your pants. Slowly."

His instructions were precise, and her compliance was instant. Turning from him, she inched the fabric down her hips, letting her pajama bottoms pool at her feet. She felt the curves of her ass peek from below the flannel shirt. She swore she could feel the heat of his gaze on it.

"Stay there," he said low.

She sucked in a shuddering breath, holding it as she waited.

"Breathe, kitten."

Her exhale came out with a giggle. Being around Jake was the only time in her life she'd needed a constant reminder to simply breathe.

The tinkling and swooshing noises of the cappuccino maker

filled the air, along with the heavenly scent of java. There she stood, bare-assed, breathing, and filled with so much anticipation, she could burst at any moment.

"Now, the top," he said, still working the machine.

She unbuttoned the flannel and dropped it to the floor. The whirring of the frother slowed. She waited patiently through the sweet torture.

He didn't touch her, but the heat of his body radiated. He was so close, she could practically taste him.

"Do you like the way this feels? Waiting? Wondering what's coming next?"

"Yes." Her reply was instantaneous.

"Then make it last. Satisfying you is now my job. Your sweet hands and the showerhead are off-limits. Let me give you what you need." From the base of her neck, his finger traced her spine, forcing a tender cry from her throat. "And you'll tell me anything and everything you want. Share your fantasies. I want to know you, kitten. Discover you. Understand?"

She could only nod.

"Turn around, Kathryn."

Her nude body slowly pivoted back to him.

Oh.

My.

God.

Capturing her gasp in her hands, she drank in the buck-naked body of Jake Russo. Technically, she'd seen his body before. But not like this.

Her thirsty gaze drank in his bold and beautiful flesh, taking a candy-land journey over his ripped and rugged body. She paid little attention to the scars she knew were from bullets. Her sights were set on the lick-worthy destination of his jutted howitzer, targeting her without mercy. She took an extra-long blink, closing her eyes to remind herself sternly, *His eyes are up there!*

She opened them to find her mug of coffee held before her face, froth still intact.

"I'll take care of your clothes. Take as much or as little time as you want in the shower, and be ready to be thoroughly dazzled by my cooking."

His sugary-sweet smile sipped again from his own mug as his eyes peered over the rim, twinkling with dirty delight.

Cupping her mug with both hands, she sashayed away.

Gliding her feet along the floor was less for sex appeal and more as part of a silent prayer that she'd be able to make it across the room and up the stairs without toppling over or spilling a steaming-hot drop.

CHAPTER 17

KATHRYN

The shower stripped away Kathryn's angst from before she arrived, but couldn't wash away all her emotions. Despite the extra second her hand spent bathing the source of her throbbing desire, her tawdry little fingers tore away, refusing to finish the job.

They know who's in charge.

Refocusing her interests, she was back to the same question nagging at her from the night before. Why was someone targeting her? Toying with her? Trying to scare her?

She worked the shampoo into her hair. Forgetting about her still tender bump, she winced. Taking a deep breath, she resumed working the suds to a lather.

Damn asshole. You can't scare me. Just piss me off.

In her prior life, she'd deployed in a battle rhythm of *six months on, six months off* for years. Her travel destinations included some of the most dangerous terrorist hot spots in the world.

Danger never deterred her. The senseless loss of losing one life after the other did. But she'd be damned to have survived multiple combat deployments just to be killed in her own home by a psychopath.

Whoever clubbed her might not have wanted her dead, but only because they didn't know who they were dealing with. Kathryn was ready for a fight—to tackle the bastards head on.

No more playing around. At least, not with a jackass who fights dirty.

Recharged and ready to work, she rinsed off. Catching herself taking a little too long with the showerhead, she shut off the water and cracked a smile.

I need to save the playing around for my dirty Dom.

Strolling downstairs in jeans, a soft blue T-shirt, and a fuzzy oversized sweater, she breathed in the aroma of bacon and eggs, which whipped her into a whole new level of submission.

Hot guy.

Sizzling bacon.

McMansion on a hill.

Just slap my ass and call me kitten.

She headed into the kitchen to find it empty.

"Out here," Jake called, his chipper tone ringing through.

She followed his voice to a sunroom flooded with soft natural light, the result of floor-to-ceiling windows on three sides. The room overlooked the woodland terrain, a backdrop of mountains and trees with a small, winding trail that traveled next to a brook. Tall grasses waved with the breeze, and a variety of wildflowers burst throughout the landscape in clusters of purple, orange, and gold.

Kathryn squealed at the sight of a red fox making its way across the wilderness that Jake called a back yard.

He gestured to the redwood chair next to him at a glass-topped table. "Here, this is a great seat to take it all in."

Her butt hit the chair as she noticed the spread. The round

table overflowed with enough food for a party of eight, and she smiled at him. "I hope you're not challenging me to an eating competition, because I am hungry. And competitive."

He beamed back with a charming, devilish double-dare of a grin. "Tempting, but in all fairness, I'd need to work up your appetite more before an undertaking like that."

Deal.

Kathryn grabbed a biscuit, but only picked at it as her mind took a turn toward work. "Look, I can't even begin to tell you how much I lo—"

His wide eyes met hers, stopping her mid-sentence—as if she was about to unleash the *L*-word.

"Uh . . . how much I love *this*. All of it. Everything you've done for me."

"A *but* is coming. Hand it over." He lowered the toast he held, forgoing a bite to give her his full attention.

"But something serious is going down, and I need to get to work. I really need to find out what's happening. As much as I'd like to spend the day—"

The chimes of the doorbell made Jake pop to his feet. He lifted a piece of bacon just shy of her mouth. She looked up, her lips automatically opening to take the bacon in her teeth.

"Hold that thought?" he asked, waiting for her nod before snatching a few strips for himself, chomping on them as he left the room.

Within minutes, she heard footsteps drawing near with the rumble of several male voices, one of which she recognized.

Surprised, she stood up as they entered. "Mr. Wolff?" She extended her hand, eager to shake that of her boss.

He took her hand in both of his. "Seriously, Kathryn? It's been three years. When are you going to start calling me Zach?"

"Not anytime soon," she told him as two other men strolled into the room.

They all sat down. Her boss, and everyone else, passed the

blueberry muffins and poured orange juice, making themselves so much at home, this couldn't be the first time.

"What are you doing here?" she asked.

Zach took a sip of orange juice and set down his glass. "Let's just say that Jake and I team up every now and again. Remember the Hartford case last year? And the crazy tip that turned the tides and helped us close the case?"

Her *yes* lifted out like a curious question. Jake raised his hand like a schoolboy, along with an irresistible eyebrow.

"*You* got us that break?" Kathryn asked, beyond shocked as he handed her a plate of pastries. Perplexed, she took the fattest chocolate chip muffin calling her name and then passed the plate along.

That investigation had stymied her for months, leading her down one messy, winding, dead-end path after another, as people in power tried to shut her down.

The case had crossed five states, stumping everyone, including the Feds. But out of the blue, they'd caught a break—a trail of cyber footprints giftwrapped and hand-delivered to their doorstep. The evidence pointed straight to a corrupt politician. Without the tip, they'd still be scratching their heads over the tangled web.

"Kathryn," Jake said, "it wasn't just me. Let me introduce you to some of my team, John Briscoe and Ben Edwards."

The two men waved at her across the pile of food, and Jake continued.

"I brought everyone together because your instincts were right. I checked your laptop. It's loaded with spyware and a keylogger. They'd wait until you logged in, then follow you around your system and record your every step. Not the highest technology on the market, but no cake walk for an amateur."

Ben cut in. "We'd like you to access your existing file. Run through your standard movements, but we'll partition you off.

Make sure you don't go anywhere sensitive. We'll guide you, because we're laying a trap to see what this is really about."

"I can do that, but . . ." Kathryn threw a worried glance at Zach.

"Speak your mind," her boss told her. "In this group, we've got no secrets."

Jake coughed to cover a chuckle. She lightly kicked him under the table, then caught the look in his eyes. Dark, but playful. Apparently, she'd committed an act that was worthy of punishment. *Finally*. She smothered her excitement. In front of her boss, she kept her game face steady.

"There is a case I've been working on lately, but I'm not sure I want to dig into it if someone's tracking my online footsteps."

Jake jumped in. "Can you walk us through what you've got? We can probably tailor a snare that would work perfectly without compromising your case."

CHAPTER 18

JAKE

Jake noticed everything about Kathryn. Her determination. Her sweetness. But he worried about her hesitation.

She trusts us. So, why is she struggling?

With a reassuring press to her shoulder, he asked, "What do you need?"

The tight line of her mouth relaxed. "I . . . uh . . . do you all mind if I pace? It comes from years of being on my feet as a nurse. I do my best processing on the move."

No one seemed terribly concerned with the request. She smiled her thanks to Jake and stood, making slow strides back and forth across the length of the room.

Before him, she transformed. Certain. Determined. Hardly the kitten begging for what he might bestow. This was the side of Kathryn Chase the world knew. The woman who had saved his life.

I could watch her all day.

As she continued to pace, his thoughts flashed to the memory of her bare skin. Her gorgeous body was branded on his mind.

With every turn, the morning light pouring through the floor-to-ceiling windows reflected off her hair in strange and fascinating ways. It cast an almost strawberry-blonde coloring with one turn, then looked distinctly honey blond at the next. It perfectly mirrored the contrasts in her character, and the inseparable differences that defined her to the core.

Wearing barely a trace of makeup, she was exposed. The other men at the table couldn't take their eyes off the unmasked woman, but they'd never know the real her.

The one who was his.

"Anyway," she said, working the puzzle aloud, "there are these three life insurance cases I've been checking for fraud. Different states. Different time frames. No connection whatsoever, except for three seemingly unrelated pieces. First, each case involved a service member who died in combat. Sadly, that's not surprising in and of itself. Service members are put in hazardous situations . . . it goes hand in hand with being military. Second, all the service members were men, which again, is not surprising. Female populations in all branches of the military are less than twenty percent, except for the Air Force. So, that all three cases had male insureds may just be a result of probability. Finally, and the most disturbing piece of the puzzle, is that all of the service members were significantly overinsured."

Jake sat back in his chair. "What's the significance of being overinsured?"

Kathryn shared an unsettled glance with Zach, who answered for her.

"Statistically speaking, overinsured people die quicker."

Silence settled in, seeming to weigh on them all.

"But again," Kathryn said, "in and of itself, maybe that's not surprising. When service members deploy, they may want to take extra precautions. You know, just in case. All I really had was, well, a hunch. My research was starting to gain momentum when I was robbed. So, I'm at square one and a half. My laptop is monitored. My notepad's in my car. It'll take me days to recreate everything I have."

"Well," her boss said with a small grin, "if you could try to call me Zach every once in a while, I might have a little something awesome for you. I'll get your new laptop. It's in the car."

"Thank you, *Zach*," she said with an extra helping of sweetness, and he left the room.

Ben set down his coffee to ask a question. "Kathryn, did you talk about the cases with anyone? Anyone at all?"

Jake nodded to himself, suppressing his smile. *Ben is the best. Waiting until Zach left before tossing her a hard-hitting question without throwing her under the bus. That man's getting a bonus.*

But as she'd confided to Jake, Kathryn was adamant that this, like her other investigations, was completely under wraps.

Ben followed his question with another standard query. "What about someone you might have needed information from?"

Her eyes widened, and she nodded slowly. "Yes. There were a few, actually. I try to stay vague with my questions, and normally I keep from mentioning my company, but I have to disclose my identity when dealing with anyone official. Or with the military."

Jake watched, frowning as her brows knitted. After everything she'd been through, this was the first time he'd really seen her worried.

She glanced around the table with a slightly sheepish look. "I contacted three separate UMOs."

"What's a UMO?" Ben asked as Zach returned with the laptop.

Zach jumped in to answer that one. "That's a Unit Movement Officer, the poor SOB who decides who's going on what deployment. A UMO will manage everything from who, when, how long . . . all that good stuff. Why?"

Jake took Kathryn's hand and squeezed. "Give us the names of the people you reached out to. We'll see who might have been in the area."

Kathryn stayed cautious. "But that still doesn't exactly connect the dots. I mean, so people are getting big insurance policies just before they deploy? That's not a crime. And somehow, a UMO, or more than one, are involved. It's not just hard to believe they'd somehow be tied together, but there's also a question of motive. Why? They're not the beneficiary."

"Well," Jake said, "the first step happens to be our specialty. Our boss, Mark Donovan, built Excelsior/Centurion to be the best of the best at what we affectionately call step one."

Jake glanced at his teammates, and they chanted in unison, "Follow the money."

CHAPTER 19

KATHRYN

Jake's home became an operations center, with the team expanding when three more men arrived. Everyone made themselves at home. Even her.

At the end of each day, Jake's kisses sent quakes straight to her core. But not much more happened than that. Was he giving her space to recover? Or keeping the focus on work?

He can't possibly think I'm holding on to that ridiculous hard limit. Perhaps a casual sub-to-Dom talk is in order when he has time for a break.

Kathryn worked casually from the kitchen bar. No matter how dedicated these guys were, two destinations were inevitable: the bathroom and the kitchen.

Camping outside the bathroom might get her slapped with an ad hoc restraining order. But the kitchen was fair game. And one of her favorite places in any house.

The social butterfly side of her got the rare privilege of chatting it up with some of the finest minds in information technology. These guys were goofy and funny, bashful and brilliant. Lucky for her, a few of the guys seemed just as starved as she was for the day-to-day human contact that was missing in the isolated world of teleworking.

I miss this. Being part of a team.

The only man she hadn't seen so far had been Jake. Most days he'd have taken a few breaks by now. But the lack of Russo sightings piqued her curiosity. Her legs were begging for a stretch, and no better time than the present.

Moseying throughout the various offices and rooms on the first floor came up Jake-less. She skipped up the stairs, finding him in the hall, dressed down more than usual in sweatpants, a T-shirt, and running shoes.

"Heading to the gym?" she asked.

He swept his hand around the small of her back, pulling her in for a warm kiss. "Just want to get a quick run before the sun goes down. I need to clear my head."

His subtle thumb strokes along her spine were enticement enough for her body to press against him harder. Her eyes closed as another kiss descended on her lips.

"Hey," he murmured against her mouth, "do you run?"

∽

Kathryn was a decent endurance runner. But as their feet pounded along the dirt trail that wrapped through the woods on his property, she could hear the obvious difference in their steps. "You don't have to do that," she panted out as she wiped sweat from her brow.

"Do what?" he said with a chuckle.

"It's like you're a cheetah pacing itself with a gimpy zebra. Seriously, I'd love to see you take off."

"No way," he said, barely huffing or breaking a sweat. "I have to keep an eye on my gimpy zebra. Make sure no one feasts on her before I do. Besides, I'm dying to know what you've figured out."

What are you, a mind reader too? That would explain a few things.

"What makes you think I've figured anything out?"

"You came looking for me."

"Maybe I missed you."

"No doubt about that, kitten. But I get the sense you wanted to share something with me. Or bounce something off of me. If it's the latter, fingers crossed it's your breasts."

She laughed at the middle-school remark. "You're right."

"It is your breasts? Yes! The fellas might be watching, but I know a little spot right behind those pines." He nudged her elbow and winked.

"Seriously, I've got something else to bounce off you." Her voice trailed off.

"Look, you can lay it on me. And that's a standing invitation for your breasts too."

Kathryn stopped running, planting her hands on her hips and bending over slightly as she caught her breath. "What I'm about to say might sound crazy . . ."

"Crazy sounds interesting," he said, encouraging her to walk so she could cool down.

As they strolled, her mind spun.

"I was thinking about motive. The UMO would have no advantage. At all. But then I started to think of this like insider trading. When people know what's going to happen to a stock before the rest of the world does, they can bet big and rake in the winnings. What if the UMO had their own insider trading?"

Jake shook his head. "I'm not following."

"Bear with me. What if the UMO knew a soldier was having issues with their spouse. Some spouses will do almost anything to get out of their marriage."

"Okay, so they file for divorce."

"Yes, they file for divorce. But in some states, filing for divorce becomes a long, drawn-out process, extending to an exhaustive level if the service member deploys. Most courts will automatically freeze the proceedings. So, instead of filing for divorce, they—"

He stopped dead in his tracks. "They take out a major life insurance policy and the soldier gets sent to a high-risk deployment. Everyone rolls the dice on the poor bastard dying."

"I don't know for sure this is the situation. It's just—"

"A hunch. I know."

He stared off in the distance, turning away from her. She wrapped her arms around him from behind, hugging hard, and he stacked his warm hands over hers.

"Kathryn, you're hesitating again. Must be something you know I won't want to hear."

Swallowing hard, she sighed. "Dominguez."

Releasing his hands, Jake tried to step away, but she held him tighter. His head tilted toward her, but his body didn't move.

His voice turned cold. "What did you find?"

"Just his name. And a loose association. And . . ." She couldn't say the words. When his body tensed in her hold, she released him. "Jake—"

"You're right." He took a few steps away. "I need a run. I'll meet you back at the house."

Without another word, he dashed down a trail and into the thick cluster of trees, disappearing into the woods.

CHAPTER 20

KATHRYN

Where is he?

The hours ticked by at a snail's pace since the team had left. Kathryn had long ago fixed dinner for the two of them, kept it warm, then finally wrapped everything up and put it away when Jake still hadn't returned. The darkness of evening cast wave after wave of worry over her, crashing down stronger as the minutes ticked by.

What if he's hurt?

Considering they were on a wooded hilltop in the middle of nowhere, anything was possible. She stepped out on the balcony, scanning the area. Except for twinkling city lights in the far-off distance, the grounds were pitch-black. She heard a faint howl.

What the hell was that?

Panicked, she headed into the house and straight to the garage.

Going out after him in the dark woods is idiotic. Insane. And sure to make me the next meal for that howling chupacabra.

But it was, without a doubt, her only choice.

Deciding she needed a flashlight, she rummaged through the

garage cabinets. When she came up empty, she cursed under her breath.

I need something. A miner's hat will do. Good grief, I'd settle for a flaming torch right now. And let's add bread crumbs to the list.

Finally, she came across something she could use.

Good. A first aid kit.

She grabbed it and continued to pilfer. The stainless-steel cabinets were fully stocked with supplies for cars, construction, and things that looked like mountain-climbing gear.

"Jesus, how many ropes does a man need?"

Spotting a pair of extreme-looking goggles, she grabbed them, turning them this way and that, then held them up to her eyes.

Maybe these are night-vision goggles. How the hell do NVGs work?

"They won't work in the light."

Jake's husky voice startled her and she whirled around, relieved when he caught the NVGs she'd dropped in her surprise.

His eyes were hard and cold. His hands were covered in blood. And his tone was unmistakably dark.

"What are you doing here, Kathryn?"

CHAPTER 21

JAKE

An hour earlier

Jake could have run several hours more, but not in the dark. And as soon as he slowed, they were there again—the litany of thoughts and emotions that terrified him.

Anxiety.

Anger.

Hatred.

Guilt.

Mostly guilt.

The woods seemed to darken, close in, and he stumbled to a stop and hung his head.

I was right. All that time, I was fucking right. I know what she's not saying. It's my fault. I should've taken the shot.

His fists flew out, pounding the trunk of a mammoth tree. He landed blow after blow until he finally dropped to his knees. Everything went numb.

He couldn't see his hands. But deep down, he knew he'd done

enough damage, because he couldn't really feel them anymore. His hands. His mind. His heart.

Relieved, he filled his lungs with air.

His mind was blank, then rested.

Better.

He wasn't sure how long he'd been there, and he didn't care. In a strange wide-awake sleepwalk, he headed home. Toward the edge of the woods, he could see Kathryn. Looking out.

Looking for me.

His head dropped. With the glow of lights from the house, he could see the raw condition of his hands. Blankly, he stared at them. When he looked up again, she was gone.

Jake entered the house, finding his cell on the kitchen counter next to Kathryn's. As soon as he unlocked it, six messages from her lit the screen. He didn't read them, just looked at the time.

It's late.

When did I leave?

Refocusing, he clicked over to the security system app. The last motion detected other than his was in the garage. Struggling to see the video feed, he blinked hard, his eyes burning from dryness.

She seemed to be rummaging through the cabinets. Finding his stash of a few choice souvenirs from his life as a Dom.

His temper flaring, he stalked into the garage. Devoid of feeling, he watched her fumble with his night-vision goggles.

"They won't work in the light."

She jolted and whipped around, dropping the NVGs, which he caught. A nudge of protectiveness surfaced at seeing her startle, and then it was gone.

"What are you doing here, Kathryn?"

CHAPTER 22

KATHRYN

*K*athryn took a second, calming herself. "God, you scared me. I was trying to find something to help me see in the dark so I could find you. Make sure you were all right." After an awkward moment locking eyes with his blank stare, she asked, "Are you? All right, I mean?"

Her gaze fell to his hands. His knuckles were bloody and cut, swollen, and practically mangled. Reacting out of instinct, she tore open the first aid kit, setting it on a nearby workbench while she took one of his hands to assess the damage.

He yanked it back. His voice lowered, darkening the words from his lips. "It's fine. *I'm* fine. Go to bed." He secured the goggles in the cabinet she'd taken them from and slammed the door, sending an echoing crack through the room.

Stunned, she took a step back, determined to steady her nerves. *Go to bed? What the hell?*

"As soon as I treat that hand. Then you can have all the space you want." She reached for his hand again, and he swung it away, towering over her.

"You need to go. *Now*, Kathryn." His loud words trembled the air, dying down to an uncomfortable silence between them. Anguished, he looked away. "An angry Dom is dangerous."

"An angry Dom is dangerous?" she repeated, disbelief fueling her own emotions. "Well, *Master* Jake, right here, right now, I'm not your sub. And since you don't want a nurse, even though you obviously need one, you're right. I should go. Because if I'm not safe with you, you've just found *my* deal breaker." Abandoning any hope of salvaging the situation, she raced away before the waterworks sprang free.

Wiping her face, she unblurred her vision, but couldn't stop more tears from squeezing through.

Keep it together. He's not worth it. He's just a . . . mistake. Another macho jerkoff masquerading as a nice guy.

A moment later, she was back in her room, blindly shoving her belongings in her overnight bag as quickly as she could.

"Goddammit," she said with a huff. Her cell in hand, she gave it a blank stare.

How can I call a Lyft? I don't even know where the hell I am. There's a gate, and a driveway eighty miles long.

She scrolled back and forth, trying to figure out her next move. Her thumb stopped at the listing for Z. WOLFF.

Nothing beats making an impression on your boss like airing the mess of your dirty laundry.

Everyone has relationship issues, right?

Screw it.

I'll break the ice by calling him Zach.

Her thumb hovered over his number, but she froze at the light knocking at her open door. She looked up, and there Jake stood, lurking like a vampire waiting to be invited in. She turned away.

"You're not safe out there," he said, glancing at her bag as he stepped into her room.

"Apparently, I'm not safe in here either, so it doesn't really matter, does it?" Using the sleeve of her shirt, she wiped the wetness rolling down her cheeks.

His hand landed lightly on her shoulder, shooting her to a whole new stratosphere of anger. Her sharp shrug pushed him away.

"Don't." Her voice was stern, and louder than she'd intended. She stewed in the surreal irony. She hadn't raised her voice in years. The last time was also because of him.

Jake held his fist over the bed and opened it, dumping a cluster of key fobs. As far as she could tell, every vehicle in the garage was accounted for.

"Take whatever you need. Or, if you'll let me, you stay here and I'll stay at your place. Or a hotel. I can't be the reason something happens to you."

She turned her head away, not meeting his eyes. "Something we agree on."

Heading out, he paused briefly to say, "Good night, Kathryn."

Good-bye, Jake.

Looking back at her cell, she knew what to do. She typed a quick text.

KATHRYN: I need your help. Where am I? Address wise.

Relieved to see bouncing bubbles, she waited for a reply. What came through didn't help. Numbers. Letters. Little degree symbols.

KATHRYN: What the hell is this?
PACO: Coordinates. Jake's place is off the grid. Intentionally. Pop those into Google Maps. Everything okay?

No. God-awful. Everything's shit and I've got to get out of here.

KATHRYN: Yes. Fine. I appreciate it. Coffee's on me next time you're in town.

She ended her text with a thumbs-up emoji for effect.

PACO: It's a date.

She cut and pasted the coordinates into a new text.

KATHRYN: It's Kat. Need you. Meet me here. Now. Put coordinates in Google Maps. I'll meet you at the gate.

Zipping up her overnight bag, she didn't wait for a reply. After perusing the assortment on her bed, she grabbed the keys to the truck. Making her way to the garage, she was grateful not to accidentally bump into Jake on the way out.

Her heart in her throat, she zoomed out of the garage in the exact same truck she'd arrived in. At least, to the gate. The proximity trigger opened the gate as soon as she was within a few feet of it. She waited impatiently in the truck, so full of roiling emotions, she didn't know how to feel.

A car eventually rolled up, making her glad he'd taken as long as he did. She'd cried herself out and was ready to rock it with a man who was fun and free, and promised a good time wherever he went.

Tossing her bag in the trunk and hopping in the front seat, she gave him a huge hug. "This girl needs a drink, and you're the only man I want to see right now."

Julian smiled through his concerned expression, taking off as soon as her seat belt was secure. "Your emergency kit is in its usual place, Ms. Kat. You want to explain why you used your ICE name?"

From under the seat, she pulled out a bag filled with mini bottles of assorted liquors. Without looking, she grabbed one, cracked open the cap, and downed its contents. "It was an emergency. *In case of emergency*, I need a wingman. I knew if you saw that name, you wouldn't blow me off. No matter how hot your date was."

"Eh." Julian shrugged. "He wasn't that cute. And that's a serious smoke signal, only to be used in dangerous situations. If you've killed someone, robbed a bank, or accidentally OD'd on buttercream frosting. That being said, you want to talk about it?"

Another bottle in, she said, "Nope." Followed by, "Shit!"

"What?"

"I left my laptop. Mr. Wolff just gave it to me, and I can't ask him for another one. We have to turn around. Good news is I left the gate open."

"Done," he said, flipping a U-turn and heading back.

∽

Kathryn entered the house with Julian on her heels. He trailed behind her, scanning the interior of the luxurious cabin, and huffed out an awe-filled, "Damn."

With a demanding motherly tone, she frowned at him as she said, "Don't make noise and don't get lost. I'll be back in two seconds."

She raced upstairs, grabbed her laptop, and was back downstairs in two shakes. Frustrated that Julian had already wandered off, she texted him.

"I'm up here," he shouted down.

Annoyed for a million different reasons, she blew a much bigger gasket when she realized he was in Jake's room.

I'm going to kill him.

Her mental swearing stopped when she heard, "Kat!" Alarmed, she bolted upstairs.

Julian hovered over Jake's unconscious facedown body, doing a quick check before slowly rolling him over. She dropped beside him, helping to move Jake gently to his back. Checking his pulse, she stared at the distinct wrinkling of his lips.

"Dehydrated."

Julian nodded. "Severely. But his hands—"

"No, that's not related to this."

He shot her a quizzical glance. "Drugs?"

She paused, looking away. "I . . . don't know."

His hand squeezed hers. "Hey, no judgment. Ambulance?"

"No."

"Off the books, it is." Quickly, he pulled his cell from his pocket and placed a call. "Jules and Kat need Thelma and Louise. We need whatever IV bags of saline you can grab. A starter kit. Pain meds, antibiotics, and a tox screen. And medical records for Jake—"

"Jacob Russo," Kathryn said.

"Jake or Jacob Russo. I'm texting you some crazy bullshit code, but if you put it in Google Maps, it'll take you right to us. Just pass the truck and go up the hill." He hung up. "They're on their way."

"Thank you," she said, not taking her eyes off Jake.

CHAPTER 23

JAKE

Groggy, Jake pried his eyes open when he heard a man sing, "Morning, sunshine."

Confused, he looked around. His room, he recognized. But the fully dressed man lying next to him wasn't ringing a bell, though he seemed friendly enough. The man rolled toward him, propping his head lightly on his hand and speaking volumes with his glee-filled eyes.

"Julian?" Jake mumbled. "What . . ." He looked down at himself, then the line leading up to a hanging bag of saline. "How long have I been out?"

"Three days," Julian said, and when Jake shot him a worried look, he rolled his eyes. "Fine. Ten hours. At least, from the time we found you."

"We? Kathryn." Jake flung his hand to his face, suddenly noticing the fresh bandages. "Where is she?" he asked, now preoccupied with admiring the coverings of both hands.

"Making a mess of your kitchen with Dana and Laurie."

Jake peeked below the blanket. "Julian?"

"Yes?" he sang, his tone way too naughty for the occasion.

"I'm naked."

"Yup."

"And clean."

"Right again."

With trepidation punctuated by a gulp, Jake had to ask, "You?" and then quickly added, "Not that I'm not grateful."

"Oh?" Julian scooted closer. "How grateful?"

"Easy, tiger. Not that grateful."

Frowning, Julian hopped off the bed. "Too bad, because we all pitched in. Just four girls washing a tank."

Jake kept on his game face. *It's just medical. They're professionals.*

"A hot, steamy tank with all the right equipment."

Okay, hot-blooded professionals.

"Kathryn's a very, *very* lucky girl." Julian winked. "And she kept your jibbly bits hidden the entire time. She insisted on polishing the old beaver-basher herself."

Shaking his head, Jake laughed. "Wow. I'm not sure I'll ever look at it again without hearing those words." Before Julian could leave, Jake said, "Thanks for wrapping my hands."

Curiosity lifted Julian's brow. "What makes you think it was me?"

"These," Jake said as he held out his hands, "were done by someone who works in plastics. And you, my smooth and wrinkle-free friend, have just the perfect skin to mean one thing."

Julian nodded. "Lead plastic surgery nurse at the best damn clinic in the state. At your service." He smoothed his hand across his jaw. "Perfect skin, huh? Smart. Charming. Built like a lord of the underworld. No wonder Kathryn loves you."

Smiling to himself, Jake closed his eyes, overthinking absolutely everything and afraid to believe it. *She loves me?*

There was barely a knock before Dana and Laurie swarmed him. One took his pulse while the other pressed a hand to his forehead. Hating to point out the obvious, he said, "I'm pretty sure I don't have a fever."

Julian jumped in. "Oh, they're just looking for excuses to touch you."

Jake threw a concerned look at Kathryn, who set a tray of breakfast on the bed beside him.

"Don't give me those terrified puppy-dog eyes," Kathryn said with a warning look. "They saved your life. Letting them paw you is a cheap price to pay."

The girls each rubbed an arm. Amused, he relaxed his arms behind his head, giving them a better gun display to manhandle.

"All right, all right," Kathryn said loudly, shooing them away. "The man's paid his debt. That's enough."

"Fine." Dana huffed, feigning a mighty big eye roll.

"We're glad you're all right," Laurie said with a smile.

Jake held Kathryn's gaze until the click of the door closing clued them both in that the trio had left.

"I can remove the IV if you like," she said.

He extended his arm.

With a gentle touch, Kathryn removed the IV, and bandaged him with a soft caress.

He rubbed her hand. "Did you just save my life again?"

Shyly, she shrugged. "Technically, Julian found you."

"How did Julian find me?"

"It's a long story."

Jake slid over, giving her room to sit beside him. "I like long stories." When she finally sat down, he pulled her tightly to him.

"I like long stories too." She sighed, snuggling in his hold. "You can tell me anything."

"I know I can." Unsure where to begin, Jake started with the name that triggered him. "Dominguez," he said slowly, trying to hold the name in reverence.

Kathryn nodded against his chest but said nothing.

"He was my commanding officer. We'd become as close as brothers. We always had each other's backs . . . until that day. The day you saved me was my last day in the Army. Not just because of the medical discharge, but because I couldn't do it anymore. I thought I saw something, something I couldn't have seen. In the heat of an attack, adrenaline pumps. Your senses are heightened. Alert. And then I saw it, just before all the gunfire exploded. One of our guys . . . turning his weapon on Dominguez."

Taking a deep breath, Jake said, "I aimed my rifle right at the man's heart. Both he and Dominguez turned to me, staring as if they thought I'd snapped. Then the gunfire started. I was still stunned, wasn't fast enough. I was hit, but I kept firing, taking hit after hit until I couldn't shoot anymore."

He squeezed her tighter. "The only thing that kept me going, making me fight to survive, was knowing that Dominguez was fine. He'd survived. But . . . I was right. Wasn't I?"

Again, she nodded.

"There was a policy on Dominguez. And they weren't going to let him go. When I didn't hear from Dominguez after my discharge, I thought he was uncomfortable. Didn't want the association of a loose cannon. But he's gone, isn't he?"

Kathryn's warm tears dropped onto his chest. "Yes. Combat. He was sent on a back-to-back deployment. Killed in combat."

"So I could've saved his life. If I'd just taken out that cocksucker when I had the chance."

"And you'd have been dishonorably discharged. And probably jailed." Kathryn wiped her tears and sat up, staring hard at him. "You couldn't have known. It was just—"

"A hunch," he said. Solemn, he stroked her hair. "I could never completely trust my instincts after that, no matter how right I thought I was. And now I . . ." He looked at the bandages around his hands. "Pain has been my go-to for a long time. My escape. A way for me to push myself until I'm numb. It's a lot to deal with. I understand if it's too much."

She lightly stroked the dressing around his hands. "It is a lot to deal with ... . alone." She slid her arms around him and gave him a tight hug. "You don't have to deal with it alone. I'm here. No judgment."

Skeptical, he asked, "You'd stay? Even knowing this is part of who I am?"

Kathryn sat up and scooted away, giving him a stern look. "For big runs, I'll strap a CamelBak on you. Dehydration solved. But when you do whatever the hell it is you did to your hands, you'll let me treat you. I'm a nurse—it's part of who *I* am. Okay?"

He looked away, uncertain how to break the news to her. Shaking his head, he said, "I don't know."

"You don't ... know?"

Holding his hands toward her, he explained. "I sort of got used to Julian's touch. What can I say? He spoiled me." He watched her hard gaze melt into a tender laugh. "Can I take these off? And shower?"

"Let's take a look." From the nightstand that had become a makeshift nursing station, she reached for the medical shears. After a few snips, she slowly peeled back the bandages. "Wow."

Prepared to lighten the worst of what she was seeing, he said, "Don't worry. It's nothing. I've had much worse."

"Actually, it looks remarkable compared to last night. Fast healing must be your superpower."

Caressing her cheek, he said, "According to Dana, my kisses are." His mouth descended on Kathryn's, grateful for her welcoming lips.

When he finally released her, she bit back a smile. "She's right." As she unbandaged the other hand, Kathryn pointedly asked, "Want to tell me what the hell happened, soldier?"

He smirked. "I might've had a knock-down, drag-out fight with a tree."

Wadding up the bandages, she stood. "Did you learn your lesson?"

"Yes, ma'am. My first and last ass-kicking by a Douglas fir. Next time I'll keep my fighting to river birches."

She discarded her handful in the bathroom. Upon returning to the bedroom, she found him standing, staring hard at her.

"You're in the same clothes you were last night."

CHAPTER 24

KATHRYN

Kathryn froze beneath the power of Jake's gaze. That and his bare-naked Adonis assets in all their glory. With a single step, he closed the distance between them, and she looked up to his darkening eyes.

"Yes," she whispered, and then firmed her voice. "I was with you most of last night. Until your favorite nurse started whining about food."

Jake reached behind her, tugging her ponytail free. "You need a shower." Before she could respond, he'd stripped off her top and bra, and began tugging off her jeans.

Powerless, she tried to dissuade him. "Jake, you're recovering."

He dropped to his knees, pressing his mouth against her panties, breathing hot kisses into her sex. "Yes, and I need a nurse." Inching her panties down, he scorched her core with his tongue.

Trembling, she said, "But everyone's downstairs. And the door isn't locked."

He stood, sliding his hand to the nape of her neck and gripping. He licked her lips. "Then use your safe word. And I'll stop."

God, don't stop.

When she didn't respond, he led her into the bathroom and turned on the shower. She tested the water and stepped in, tipping her head back to allow the hot streams to wash away everything on her mind but the moment.

Jake followed and adjusted the strength of the jets. "Temperature okay?" When she nodded, he pumped shampoo in his palm and gently lathered her hair, then rinsed her hair clean. "Does this hurt?"

She shook her head, letting out a breathy, "No. But your hands..."

"They're fine."

With a handful of soap, he dedicated his hands to her body. He lathered her slowly, massaging her slick skin as her sudsy hands moved against his taut muscles.

He's beautiful. Perfect.

Her fingers slowed over every scar as she admired the body of a man whose return from hell shaped him into a god. Each wound, memorized long before this, had been sealed closed with her fingerprints.

She'd laid her claim on him years ago.

"There's something you need, kitten." His words were more than those of a man eager to plunge into her desire. This was an offer. Just for her. His fingers dipped down, sliding back and forth through the slickness of her folds.

"Y-yes," she said, her lips quivering. His hands seduced everything at once, caressing her sex and ass together.

His low voice whispered, "Say red if you need to."

With her nod, his tongue pushed through her trembling lips. As he flicked at the blooming nub of her clit with one hand, his other roaming fingers skimmed back and forth between her cheeks.

Rising to her toes and whimpering with want, she held him in as he took her to a forbidden pleasure she'd never imagined. Her breath stuttered as her nails raked across his skin.

He sighed in pleasure, coaxing her for more. "That's it, little kitten. Harder."

Her fingers curved, and she ran her nails harder across his skin. She could feel herself building, with more sensations exploding from every sweep of his hands. His teeth bit sweetly, and the tug of her nipple was too much.

"Come for me," he demanded, with a gentle finger forcing through the barrier of the sweet spot between her cheeks.

Her body shuddered as the ecstasy erupted in a throaty cry. When she collapsed back against the wall, his mouth was on hers, crashing through her open lips, hungry to swallow each moan.

He pulled back from her still wanting mouth. "More, kitten?"

Her heavy eyes met his, and she nodded.

His voice softened. "What do you want?"

She shuddered, still filled with his finger, afraid to set the words free.

"Say it," he whispered.

"You, Jake." Her finger traced his jaw. "Since the moment I laid in your arms . . . blindfolded, baring my soul and my secrets. You're what I want."

"I'll be right back."

"No," Kathryn said, still panting. "You don't need to get anything. I'm covered. And I want you. All of you."

His powerful arms lifted her, and her legs wrapped around him. His tip slid to her entry as his fingers again dipped in before he shoved the length of his shaft inside her core, stretching her in crashing waves of hard thrusts matched to the tempo of the finger working her ass.

"I—I can't breathe," she said, panting.

"Then say red," he growled.

"No," she huffed out, slicing her nails down his arms.

Merciless, he thrust her hard against the wall, forcing the length of himself deep inside before her cries echoed with his on the glass walls of the shower.

CHAPTER 25

KATHRYN

Kathryn enjoyed having breakfast with a bigger group than usual, this one decidedly more feminine than the usual gang around the table. Dana, Laurie, and Julian didn't stick around after demolishing the spread as if it were a trough. Though eager to be back in the swing of the investigation, she found concentrating on work was a lost cause.

Jake's casual wardrobe somehow made him sexier. And the way he dove into full-on operational mode made him even more attractive. *How is that even possible?* His hand rubbed her knee, and heat surged across her cheeks.

Thank God everyone's eyes were on him. She sipped her cold juice, praying she'd cool off before someone noticed her odd rosiness.

"If we can verify how they're getting their information, we can push the trap. Couples who are on the outs. Ones where there might be a big payday if the military member suddenly became deployed." Jake tore a hot muffin in two, sliding a knife of butter across the steaming half before taking a bite.

"No." Zach shook his head. "Nothing sudden about this MO.

They have to be better thought-out than that. People are being picked through. Prime candidates are decided on."

Jake picked up muffin number two. "I know it sounds unlikely, but base chaplain?"

Kathryn checked her reconstructed notes. "Doubtful. The three we know of were of different faiths. I mean, base chaplains can serve all faiths, but one service member had a strong connection with his family rabbi, so I can't see this guy dishing any marriage dirt to a stranger. That eliminates a common thread. But," she flipped further in her notepad, "yesterday I was working on building a search using the same basic premise, to see how many overinsured service members we might be talking about. I got a ton of hits. Some are easier to eliminate because the deaths, though overseas, weren't in contingency areas. And I also brought in a list of those that met all the criteria, who happen to still be alive. Cross referencing both lists, I'm up to about a hundred fifty-three, most active duty, but some reservists on active-duty status."

Ben spoke up next. He and Ed had done a divide-and-conquer on the lists of UMOs. "We've pretty much crossed one off the list because the position has been vacant. Two other UMOs were working the bases in tandem. We'll keep digging."

Zach helped himself to another croissant and asked Kathryn, "Is there anything else you need? You don't have a car right now."

She was about to accept when Jake said, "I've got a Range Rover that's all gassed up and ready to go. It's yours if you like. I can load your phone with the apps for the gate and the house."

Zach gave him a frown. "Well, hell, Jake. I'd like a Range Rover. Or the least you could do is gas up my car, since getting out here is like going on friggin' safari."

"Well, maybe," Jake said, grinning at Zach. "If you do for me what Kathryn did, we just might have a deal."

Everyone's eyes popped, Kathryn's widest of all.

"I mean," Jake said as his smile grew, "she did save my life, after all."

Everyone laughed as he gave her a playful glance.

~

As the day flew by and should have been winding to a close, Kathryn's momentum came to a screeching halt. *What the hell?* She looked through the information again. Then a third time.

Rattled at what she'd found, she searched the house, following the echoes of laughter to the largest office on the first floor. She knocked on the door frame, and all the men looked back at her.

"Hey," she said shyly. "Jake, can I steal you for a moment?"

"Sure." He stood up from his laptop and followed her outside to the large deck. "What's going on?" He caressed her shoulders, rubbing out the tension as they soaked in the sunny view and the crisp air.

"I've been refining my search, and now I have a good list of candidates. Mostly women. All likely beneficiaries." She sucked in a deep breath. "Who's Chelsea Anders?"

His hands dropped from her shoulders as he moved next to her, bracing himself against the wood railing and staring off into the distance. "Was she one of them? A beneficiary?"

Kathryn took an eternity getting the smallest word past her lips, reconsidering her initial thought of *yes*. "Maybe. I can't be certain because it looks like the final signature never happened. But the system was set up like the claim was going to be processed anyway. Technically, it looks like it had been processed, then pulled back. But I can't find policy payments. And if an insurer canceled the policy, returning any premiums paid is the industry standard. I can't find a trace of that either."

He stood up and headed back into the house. "Look, I need to check this out. Personally. Find out what happened, and—"

"I completely understand," Kathryn lied, hating that he was leaving, and full of questions.

Why can't the king of cyber investigating check on this here?
Where is this person?
Who is this person?

"I'll be back." With a quick peck to her lips, he left.

CHAPTER 26

JAKE

"I'm glad you could see me." Jake hung his Ray Bans over the neck of his T-shirt as he was ushered in through the front door.

"God, Jake, how long has it been?" Chelsea asked.

"Three years." His words came out flat.

The stunning brunette still had a body most men would do anything for. But Jake had long ago risen above the ranks of most men. As usual, her makeup was impeccable. Like a Kardashian who'd always be ready for any camera.

He stepped into the foyer. The contemporary house in the middle of suburbia was set prominently in a gated community within an upper-crust school district. "Still in real estate?" he asked, tossing out a nonchalant conversation starter.

"And loving every second of it." She strolled to the kitchen. "Can I get you a drink? I've got Gentleman Jack."

"I'll take water. Tap is fine."

With a *suit yourself* shrug, she filled a glass and handed it to him. They made their way to a large living room with expensive furnishings that were clearly oversized for the house, and too garish for his taste.

"You've done well," he said.

She sat, patting the sofa for him to join her.

Not a fucking chance.

He took a chair.

"You look amazing," she said with a giggle. "I can't believe how much you've recovered. And worked out. I'm stunned."

"Thanks, Chels. You look great." *Backstabbing must be one hell of a workout for you.*

Despite their differences—like their individual comprehension of the word *monogamy*—he sat, stunned. Up close, he still couldn't believe she'd actually try to have him killed.

He needed an answer, face-to-face.

"Funny," she said, scooting closer to his seat. "I've been thinking about you a lot, Jake. I know we had our differences."

That's a PC way to paint infidelity. Like calling a reverse harem "teambuilding."

"I just couldn't imagine how I'd deal with everything. With you. With us. And seeing you now reminds me of just how good we were together." Her hand slid to his knee. "We can have that again. The heat. We can pick up exactly where we left off."

Her fingernails clawed down his thigh to his knee as she flaunted her thick lashes and red pout.

Disinterested, he hit her with the low grumble of one word. "No."

She backed off, but knelt at his feet. Here she was, with her ass-length ponytail flipped across her shoulder, teasing him to wrap his fist around it. Now, nothing bored him more than predictability.

Pouting again, she said, "Please. I need you. I still have my engagement ring. Remember when you gave it to me?"

How could I forget? The night was twisted. Kinky. Steering him deep into the world of delicious darkness. *My first night as a Dom.*

Thinking back on it, his body heated. With rage.

"We've both moved on, Chels. I'm not interested in reliving the past."

She leaned closer, her assets nearly spilling out of her low-cut blouse. Cautiously, she touched both hands to his thighs as she licked her lips. "Not even for old time's sake?"

Not even if my dick fell off, and the only way to keep it attached was to have your lips hold it in place.

"No," hit the air like a thud.

"Then why are you here?" Despite her best efforts, the irritation in her tone rang through.

He didn't move, letting his glare project his seriousness. "Because I want to know about the life insurance policy you took out on me before my last deployment."

Snapping out of her seduction, she jumped to her feet. "I took out on you? I know what you're doing. Teasing me. Finding a way to punish me. I'll give you anything you want, Jake."

What I want. Let me think. How about the answers to:

How could you fuck my best friend the entire time I was deployed?

How the hell does a woman abandon her fiancé, leaving him for dead in the hospital?

And what kind of woman lies about being pregnant?

"Here's what I want, Chels. I want to know, in painstaking detail, everything to do with that life insurance policy. I want names, dates, emails, and phone numbers. I want to know who else was involved."

He took out his phone and pressed VOICE RECORD. "Now, start talking."

∼

Three hours later, Jake had everything he needed and stood up to leave.

"Jake, wait." Chelsea flew into his arms.

Irritated, he huffed, planting his hands on his hips.

"You want this. Us," she said.

He pushed her away, gentle but firm. Eye to eye, he said, "No. I don't."

"But you gave me all your equity in your house, when I had nothing. Why do that if you don't still have feelings for me?"

He held her at arm's length. "You don't get it. The cheating was bad enough. And ditching me in the hospital, that was a class act all on its own. But you said you were pregnant—with another man's child—and he abandoned you. We grew up together. Your folks and my folks are friends. I didn't give a damn what people thought of me, but it would reflect poorly on them. I'd do anything for them. I wasn't taking you back, and I wasn't ratting you out. This was the cleanest break I could get at the worst possible time in my life."

Blocking his way, she said, "You helped me because you love me."

"No, Chels. I helped you because I believed you when you lied and manipulated me. There was no pregnancy. None of it was true, and you thought I would never find out. Just like this policy."

The truth moved her out of the way, yet she still pleaded. "I'm sorry. I wasn't trying to get your money. I thought you would stay."

Calmly, he said, "You thought wrong."

He left, focusing on his cell as it buzzed. The security system alerted him to movement at the gate.

CHAPTER 27

KATHRYN

After spending the remainder of her day trying to stay focused on her task, Kathryn found herself alone as the day came to a close.

Again? Seriously?

The team had wrapped up and left hours ago. Since then, she'd passed the time puttering about, staying busy, tidying up and organizing things. Filling every minute trying not to obsess about some woman named Chelsea Anders.

Determined, she opened her laptop and googled the sophisticated-sounding name.

The good news? There was only one Chelsea Anders within driving distance. The bad news? She looked like a supermodel and was a top local real estate agent. The differences between them would make a lesser woman worry.

Good thing I'm so secure.
With my man.
Who's been gone for hours without a word.

Suddenly, Kathryn needed her friends.

She glanced down at her ensemble for the day. Leggings and a black tee, topped with a denim shirt. *Rodeo chic.* Meanwhile, the woman in a spokesmodel pose smiling gleefully from the laptop was decked out like she'd just shopped on Rodeo Drive.

When Kathryn made the mistake of looking further, the news article she found smacked her right in her ego. It was an old engagement announcement, slating Chelsea as the bride-to-be. The future Mrs. Jake Russo.

So, they were engaged? Big deal. It explains her being his beneficiary.

Kathryn squinted at the screen. He couldn't possibly be falling for a woman who might have tried to have him killed.

Definitely not. They've probably spent the past several hours doing . . . other things.

The little clock on her monitor yanked her attention.

Where the hell is he?

Her agitation ticked higher.

Fine. He lost track of time.

With his ex.

Who looks like a real-life Barbie.

Her fingers strummed the desk.

Fuck it.

She shut the laptop.

I've got to get out of here.

Swapping her leggings for her favorite pair of boot-cut jeans, and ditching the flannel for a lined leather jacket, she made herself comfortable in the shiny black Range Rover. She'd already called the dynamic trio. Apparently, they were rocking a long extension of happy hour without her, assuming she'd be preoccupied.

Sadly, she was. But not in the fun way they'd alluded to.

She met them for Mexican and margaritas, ordering her standard substitute of Tito's vodka for tequila. "Tequila and I broke up years ago," she explained to the waitress, "and it was a bad breakup."

"Girl, everyone breaks up with tequila," the waitress joked.

"Not me," Julian slurred. "I'm on again with that devil until she does me wrong." He sipped from his impractical fishbowl margarita that had just been delivered, stuffed with an upside-down bottle of Corona.

"Damn, boy. Tough day?" Laurie said with a giggle.

"Tough fucking week, girl. But it's about to get oh-so-much better." His lips tightened around the three straws in his drink, as if sucking it down was his God-given gift.

"Mind if I join you?" came an all-too-familiar voice from behind Kathryn.

They all looked up. She turned as well, then returned to her drink. She gave a subtle shake of her head to her friends before taking a sip.

Dana jumped in. "Sorry. It's a private party."

The man rested his hand on Kathryn's shoulder, and she stiffened. "Kathryn, I really think you should let me take you out of here."

Loud and demanding, she said, "Look, Artie, I'm sorry, but I'm just not interested."

She didn't bother looking back, already fuming that this grade-A asshole was stupid enough to put his hands on her.

"But," his hand squeezed harder, "I insist."

Oh, count me in. It's been a hot minute since my hand-to-hand combat training, and I've got a lot of pent-up steam.

Taking another sip, she was giving the son of a bitch until the count of three to remove his hand. Just the right amount of time to finish her drink.

One.

Two.

Then his hand was gone.

"Hey!" he shouted.

Jake had the guy's hand, specifically his thumb, contorted and hiked up behind his back, forcing the guy to his tippy toes before

Jake released him with a shove. "I believe the lady gave you her answer."

The guy stumbled off, leaving the restaurant.

As Jake straightened his shirt, Kathryn noticed her friends staring at the sexy hunk like they'd just ordered him off the naughty hottie menu.

Julian waggled his brows. "Well, well, well, aren't you just the smoking-hot knight in shining armor."

"Hardly." Jake smiled at Kathryn. "I didn't mean to interrupt, but I noticed your expression, and didn't want you busting out a can of whoop-ass in the middle of your meal. You're still recovering."

She stared at him, coy and calculating.

I can't stay mad at him. He's my crack-laced Kryptonite, deep-fried and covered in butter.

"What on earth makes you think I'd do that?" Her grin turned sly.

He grabbed a nearby chair, flipping it around to straddle it beside her. When a waitress came up to request his drink order, he said, "Just water."

She nodded and strolled off while he continued.

"Oh, I know. You look sweet as apple pie, but you've got a mean right hook, and I've got the medical record to prove it."

"What?" Kathryn glared at him, incredulous at his nerve. And amused.

The rest of the table egged Jake on to continue.

"Seven years ago," he said to Kathryn. "You were in a hand-to-hand combat course. Bright eyed. Bushy, um, tailed."

She giggled, stopping him there. "If I recall correctly, this was a woman-only course, and my instructor was definitely not you."

Laurie asked, "Because your instructor was a *she?*" She swung her head toward Jake. "Uh, if you've transitioned, you look a-maz-ing!"

Jake laughed, and Kathryn joined him.

"No," she said. "Captain Alfonso Roberts was a tower of power, beautiful inside and out, and distinctly black."

Julian's eyes lit, intrigued as he asked, "Do you keep in touch? Is he single?"

They all laughed as the waitress handed Jake a tall glass of water. He sipped at it, still grinning.

Captivated, Kathryn asked him, "How do you know about the class?"

"I was . . . well, your crash-test dummy."

Her face froze in amused shock. Her double-take was long and pronounced, hitting almost every part of his body. "Hang on. You? That's not possible. The guy I sparred with was, like, twelve years old and a beanpole. I even told him to—"

"Eat something," he said, finishing her sentence.

"Oh my gosh," Julian blurted. "She's always telling me the exact same thing."

Kathryn's hands flew to her face, covering her flaming cheeks. "It *was* you. Oh my God. I broke your nose." She winced at the recollection, reaching out to slide her finger over that very same nose.

"To your credit, you reset it on the spot." He wiggled it, proving its resilience. "Which hurt like hell. But it taught me a lesson. Keep my guard up, no matter how deceptively cute my opponent is. Though none of them were ever as gorgeous as you." As he took a last sip, her friends let out a collective *aww* around the table. "Listen, I just dropped by for a second. Walk me out?"

Kathryn walked out with him, his arm wrapping around the small of her back. "So, I scared you away the first time," she teased as they strolled into the parking lot.

"Well, I was scared off, all right, but it wasn't because of your right hook. More like your left ring finger. You were married at the time to a certain military surgeon we both know."

Nodding, she rubbed the band-free finger. "Fair enough."

"And if that hadn't stopped me, you were an officer. Fraternization would have stopped me cold." He stopped to reconsider. "Eh, maybe."

"Hmm, I think what might have stopped me is that I'm pretty sure back then you were technically a minor."

Jake chuckled loudly. "I wasn't that young. Last I checked, we're the exact same age."

"*Au contraire*," she said, taking the opportunity to rub his arm. "I'm positive I'm older. Even if only by a few months."

"Fine. You're robbing the cradle," he said, tenderly pressing her back against his truck and sliding his finger from her collar bone to between her breasts. His lips were a breath from hers.

"To be clear," he said softly, "you might be older, and I'm well aware you can pack a wicked punch. But if I'm around, I'm protecting you. And everyone will know you're mine."

His lips captured hers, and when he slipped his tongue inside, she sucked hard on it and pressed her body against his. He pulled away, and she shuddered.

"I didn't mean to stalk you, kitten. I got a ping on my phone as soon as the SUV left the property, and this was on my way back. I know you have questions, about Chelsea, as well as other things. And I've got some of my own. So, when you're ready, come home, and let's get to know each other better." His hands cradled her ass as he gave her one last kiss. "My way."

Breathless, she nodded.

Slipping a credit card in the back pocket of her jeans, he kissed her again. "Girls' night is on me. I owe everyone this and more." He stepped up into his truck, and rolled down the window after starting it up. "I'll watch you get safely inside. Make sure your friends walk you out. See you in a bit."

Her fingers trailed off his truck, and she headed back in.

CHAPTER 28

KATHRYN

A few hours later, Kathryn returned to the palatial compound she now called home. The lighting was dim, but not dark, lending a warm glow to the interior. Through the glass patio doors, she could see Jake leaning against the balcony wall, enjoying a drink and a cigar, and she headed out.

The perfume of whiskey and cigar smoke breezed across her, bringing back the happier highlights of her travels.

"San Cristobal?" she asked, popping the words with whimsy.

Her question was met with an impressed nod. "You know your cigars. It is. Quintessence."

"May I?" she asked, and when he nodded, her fingers lifted the cigar from his hand. Expertly, she took a few puffs, then blew out a relaxed breath.

His awestruck stare prompted her smile, and she looked up innocently.

"What? I indulge every now and then. I did some charity work in South America just before I joined the Army." She admired the cigar between her fingers before handing it back. "Good times." Her smile beamed from a girl who'd enjoyed a night or two of frivolous fun. "So, are we playing twenty questions?"

He tapped out the cigar on the outside of the railing and set it on the table before leading her back inside. His nod was declarative. "I'm game. But I'm starving."

"Sure. So you want to eat first?"

The line of his mouth curled up along with a distinctly diabolical brow. "Oh no. I'm eating *after* our game."

He led her to the oversized sofa and offered her a seat, but opted to stand. "Here's the game. You ask me a question, any question at all. The more you probe, the better. When you're satisfied I've answered your question completely, you remove a piece of clothing. And vice versa."

"And what happens when we're out of clothes?" she asked.

He took another sip of his booze, letting his darkened gaze travel over her body. "Then I eat." He polished off his drink and made his way to grab another. "Would you like one?"

"Definitely."

A moment later, he brought two glasses to the couch, placing one in her waiting hand.

"Okay," she said. "Who goes first?"

"Ladies always go first."

"Lucky me." She tried not to sound too eager. Pulling in a breath, she said, "Okay, who's Chelsea Anders?"

After a sip, he seemed to suddenly lose interest in his whiskey neat, and set down the glass.

"Chelsea Anders." His gaze drifted, staring off into nothing. "Chels was my childhood sweetheart. We were pretty much inseparable since middle school. Did everything together. Dated forever. Whole photo books filled page after page of two kids growing up side by side. We got engaged the night we graduated from high school. But between my training and deployments, we never saw each other. We broke it off after my last deployment."

He trailed off, struggling to say more.

Keeping the million and one follow-up questions to herself, Kathryn slipped off her leather jacket.

"Should I grab a coat too?" he asked.

Her face filled with mischief. "Too late. The game's already started. Your turn."

"My turn." He settled back into the corner of the sofa, his fingers woven comfortably across his torso. "Did every single thing we did in the shower turn you on?"

Her gaze dropped to her drink. Pretending to whiff the amber liquid, she tried hiding the blush rushing up her cheeks and neck. She took a large swallow and held the glass tightly to her chest as she nodded and raised her head. "Yes."

He held her gaze for a second before she looked away. Obviously satisfied, he sat up and unbuttoned his shirt, tossed it aside. "Your turn."

Her next question was tricky. She didn't want to pry, but she wanted so much more about his history with his supermodel ex.

"Hey," Jake said, pulling her out of her mental ping-pong tournament. "This is a time for us to get our cards on the table. I know you'll push my comfort zone, but I'm pushing yours too. I can take whatever you have to throw at me. Don't hold back with me. Not now. Not ever." He pulled her on his lap, suddenly serious in their game. "It's no fun if you hold back."

Her eyes searched his. Secure in his sincerity, she pressed on. "Why would Chelsea have a life insurance policy on you? She wasn't listed as your next of kin when I . . . treated you."

"How do you know that?"

Kathryn shrugged, knowing it was hopeless to keep this from him. "I checked. In case we lost you again."

He pulled her close, so her head rested on the warmth of his chest. "Chels and I were engaged, but my dad and I decided it would be best if he was my next of kin. If someone had to break the news to my mom and Chels, we both wanted it to be him. But I wasn't the same man when I returned home, and she wasn't the same girl. We'd drifted apart."

Wanting to lighten the mood, Kathryn turned playful. "So, did we each do a question?"

"Yup," he said, tugging his T-shirt off over his head, and she did the same. Then he pulled her right back into his arms. "But I'm going next. Would you like more of what I gave you in the shower?"

Just thinking about it tied her tongue, and she struggled to answer.

His hand skated down her arm, and he whispered, "Well, kitten?"

Her breath coming out in little pants, she said softly, "Y-yes."

He slipped out from her embrace and stood. As he stared down, his eyes darkened a shade from the bright hazel they were during the day. Tracing her lip with his thumb, he said, "Remove my pants."

She did. With the button free and zipper undone, his bulge broke through as his trousers hit the floor. He stayed standing. Daring, she traced the band of his briefs with a finger and caught his eyes, waiting for approval.

He nodded, and off his briefs came. When she opened her mouth, ready to take him in, he touched her hair. "Not yet. Your clothes are standing between me and my meal. You've got one last question."

"Right." She exhaled slowly, absorbed in his hypnotic rod. "Um . . ." She cleared her throat, worried she was about to spoil an unbelievably hot moment, and hating herself for it. Dropping her head, she asked, "Do you still have feelings for her?"

He grabbed Kathryn's arms, pulling her to her feet. "Not the way you think. And nothing like the feelings I have for you." His gaze dropped to her jeans. "Take off the rest of your clothes. Then I want you bending over the breakfast table. You left the house without a word."

She tried to interrupt, but he pressed a finger to her lips, sealing in her excuse.

"I was late. I didn't call or text. Your quid pro quo was deserved. But I'm punishing you anyway, unless you stop me. And afterward, I'm eating." He released her and stepped back.

Slowly, she removed her jeans.

I'm so wet.

Too wet.

He'll think I peed my pants.

Slipping the stretchy lace down her legs, she casually slid her underwear beneath her bundled jeans, hiding the evidence.

"Not so fast, little kitten. Hand them to me."

Although she didn't want to, she handed him the tight wad of soaked undies.

The breakfast nook glowed with moonlight. When she did as he asked, pressing her palms on the table, the bright beams hit her like a spotlight. He posed her, leaning her over a little more, and pulled her hips back.

"Don't move," he said, and his words locked her in place.

His hot hands explored her, rubbing up and down her thighs and ass, finally settling across her slick center. He swiped, then sucked his finger clean.

His moan was deep, and his words raspy. "I want more."

He slapped her ass—hard. Her loud whimper melted to a moan. He rubbed her ass, then spanked her other cheek even harder. Smack after heavenly smack, her waiting eruption grew.

His punishment was merciless, and her cries revealed her ecstasy. Two fingers dove deep to chase the source of her trembling. A few pumps in and he stopped, sliding his fingers out and sucking them clean of every drop of her need.

Then he rested his cock on the crack of her ass.

Just having the weight of his hard, heavy dick on her tender hole was too much. She felt new wetness dripping down the inside of her thigh, and she squirmed beneath him.

"Mmm . . . that's it. I'm ready to see my main course." With a last spank, he pulled back. "Sit on the edge of the table."

Setting a chair before her, he made himself comfortable. There he sat, hard as a rock, his elbows on the armrests, and his fingers steepled to his chin. His hungry eyes scanned her, taking in every line of her body.

"Lean back," he said. "Rest your weight on your hands."

Obeying, she slid her palms behind her, lifting her chest and trying to calm her ragged breathing.

"Put your foot here." His chin pointed to the armrest, but his hands stayed clasped together.

Doing her best Cirque du Soleil imitation, she arched her body back, lifting her leg as her foot found the arm of the chair.

He'd opened her, capturing her erotic exposure front and center.

"Now the other one."

With that, she shifted her weight to follow his instruction, instantly graduating from dancer to gymnast.

The minute her foot landed on the armrest, his fingers swiped through the moisture at the very top of her inner thigh. Her head dropped back, and she released a gasp as she shivered.

Her eyes fell shut as his lips made his way up her thighs, one hot little nibble at a time. Closer to her center, his tongue lashed her in long strokes, licking every juicy drop along her legs.

His avoiding her pussy pushed her to the brink. Her hips rocked, and her ass swiveled. But it was no use. His flaming tongue was set to torture.

Fidgeting for dear life, she clutched the edge of the table, her nails etching her frantic desire into the wood. "Please," she begged.

"Not good enough." He stopped, and his gaze locked on her wanting eyes peering through heavy lids. The tip of his finger traced the top of her thigh. "You tried hiding something from me."

Confused, she panted, barely able to breathe. "What?"

He raised her lace undies by one finger, swinging them slowly in the moonlight. "Trying to hide your sweet soaking-wet panties from me. That has earned you a day of no undies . . . and a few more minutes of this."

The heat from his finger was killing her as he tormented her. His fingertip grazed figure eights across her thighs and traced up her ass, avoiding her pleasure center.

Overcome with desire, she panted out, "I need you."

Her whimpers climbed as his tongue skimmed her, tracing a torturous path along her slit. Her back arched, and then she lifted her hips.

Grinning, he gripped her hips, holding her in place. His voice deepened with the darkness of his eyes. "I know what you need."

The heat of his breath at her entrance made a gasp shoot from her throat.

The serpentine stroke of his tongue was so strong, her body began to shudder, climbing for an orgasm way too fast. He pulled back.

"I—I . . ."

"Shh."

He massaged her hips, letting her come back down, then pressed two fingers inside her, pumping hard. Her legs draped over his shoulders as the shuddering burst from deep within.

"Come, little kitten." His tongue made its way to her clit, where his lips latched hard, pushing her to another level of bliss. Her throaty screams echoed throughout the room, stopped only by the exhaustion of her breath.

Collapsing on her elbows, she began sliding off the table. He lifted her, then set her into the chair still warm from his body. Hers wouldn't be the only orgasm that night.

He took a turn propping a foot on the armrest, as the hunger in his eyes melted to longing. When the bravest man she'd ever known wanted nothing more than her lips around his cock, the man was getting some serious deep throat, and failure was not an option.

Fisting the base of his heavy shaft, she worked his length with her lips and tongue, sweeping further down each time. But now and again, she'd come up for air, needing to take an amateur breath.

"Easy, kitten," he finally said before riding her lips to the peak of momentum. "I'm pulling out."

The hell you are.

In too deep to turn back now, she clutched his ass, keeping him locked in her mouth. He tugged her hair, capturing her eyes, but not losing his rhythm.

Gruff and low, he demanded an answer. "Is this what you want?"

Her steady sucking picked up as her fingernails grazed his butt.

She watched him, a voyeur in her own porno. His body moving was the hottest version of her every fantasy. His rapid thrusting slowed and he pulled in a breath, seeming to ride out the sensation.

Her fingers walked high up his back, teasing his skin by letting her nails sink in, then waiting. Faster, he pounded into her mouth, his grip tightening on her hair.

"Now," he cried, and she unleashed her nails deep down his body.

His release was hot in her throat, filling her with the satisfaction of knowing he was hers too.

He pulled out, lifting her shivering body into the heat of his, and carried her to bed.

CHAPTER 29

KATHRYN

The morning ritual of breakfast with the boys was a little daunting this go-round. Embarrassed, Kathryn stared at the tabletop, now scarred with several scratches. The evidence of her rapturous fingernails solidified her guilt. The little marks practically winked at her.

Don't blush.
DON'T blush.
Don't.
Blush.

When Jake speared a plump breakfast sausage and laid it on her empty plate, her smile widened to the point of a giggle. Fighting her laughter, she said, "I need to get a few things taken care of. I'll skip breakfast for now."

The excuse was good enough to tear her away from the men. Without her, she heard them continue their breakfast and chatter over the game plan for the day.

In her bedroom, she was booting up her laptop when a light knock lifted her head. Jake strolled in with a plate of a little bit of everything and a fresh coffee. Scolding him with her eyes, she sipped the steaming-hot java. He set the plate on the nightstand, and their lips lingered in a kiss before breaking off in laughter.

"Sorry, kitten," he whispered against her mouth. "I live for that gorgeous blush of yours." A few pecks later, he let her get back to work.

~

Within a few hours, everyone had circled back. The money trail and motive traced back to one name—or half a name, really. That name kept popping up in connection to several offshore accounts with upward of a few million dollars, safely divided and stashed across a few Caribbean islands.

Having money isn't a crime, Kathryn reminded herself.

Linking large wire transfers from the bank accounts of insurance beneficiaries to those accounts? Some would call it probable cause. The team considered it a hop, skip, and a jump to a slam-dunk case—*if* they could figure out the name connection. Sometimes it was a first name. Sometimes, a last name. But the same name popping up was more than a coincidence. All Kathryn knew to the depth of her being was they were making a mistake.

Aside from her hunch, she had nothing. And from the looks Jake gave her throughout the rest of the day, he wouldn't be convinced without cold, hard evidence. Maybe all she needed was one crazy-ass idea.

~

"Bait?" Jake barked the word at her. "Any scheme that involves you as bait is obviously the worst idea in the world."

His words boomed, echoing off the walls and windows of his home office. At least the door was closed. One thing Kathryn had learned about her escapade in the shower was that all the house's rooms were blissfully soundproof.

Kathryn held her ground. "I could just start bragging in small circles that I've cracked this major case. Then I make those circles bigger until we lure out the culprit."

Jake tightened his arms across his chest, teasing her with the sight of his solid biceps. "You might be tough as nails and independent as hell, but there's zero chance we're setting a trap like that around you." He relaxed into a sexy half smile. "Perhaps I need you to assume the position?"

The warmth blooming in her cheeks caught her off guard. Defiant, she planted her hands on her hips. "It won't stop me."

Grabbing her hand, he yanked her to his lap. His low grumble feathered across her neck. "Don't be so sure. I need you to stop thinking like this."

Luring her with a seductive distraction wouldn't work this time. "I've got to do something. I can't just twiddle my thumbs."

"You're not," he said, pressing a kiss to her lips. "And there *is* something nobody else can help with. Something I don't want to discuss with the others. At least, not yet."

"Carter." She said his name quietly, sinking into the feeling that a premier surgeon—and her ex-husband—could be connected with these heinous crimes.

Jake nodded. "The team coming up with it wasn't the first time I'd heard it with this case, but I didn't want to mention it until I had more to go on. I talked with Chels. The life insurance policy showed up in the mail. She doesn't remember much, but she assumed I'd initiated the policy with the tempo of my deployments. She called the phone number on the paperwork, but wasn't interested because . . . well, she'd made a decision. She knew it might be the beginning of the end for us. Anyway, she ended up throwing it away. But there were so many meetings before my deployment, the only thing she remembered about the guy she spoke to was his name. Carter."

Skeptical, Kathryn immediately challenged the recollection. "How could she possibly remember that?"

Rolling his eyes, Jake said, "She thought the name was sexy, so she called. And it stuck with her." With a pause, he pushed out, "Carter R."

She bolted from his lap. "There's no way that's possible, Jake. I was married to Carter Reeves for years. Sure, he's an arrogant asshole who thinks he's God's gift to medicine. One hundred percent. But if he were in it for the money, trust me, he wouldn't live in shitholes in the Middle East for months on end. And *Do No Harm* isn't just an oath to him. It's his life. I'm telling you . . . it's not him."

"I'm not saying it is," Jake said in a calm voice. "We need to figure this out, and we will. But in order to do that, I need your help, and not by letting you walk out the door as bait. Okay?" Staring her down, he waited for her response.

Resigned, she nodded. "Fine. I won't be bait if you don't hide things from me. Otherwise, you've earned a day of no boxers."

The arch of his brow made it clear that her terms weren't exactly a punishment. "Agreed," he said slowly, his voice low.

Needing to avoid his ridiculously alluring magnetism, she stepped away to get her mind back on track. "What else do you have?"

"Not much. Chels didn't sign anything. Someone was pre-populating forms, assuming the spouse would sign up the service member. But what's bugging me is how someone could do that without consent. I kept everything I signed, and there was nothing like this."

Kathryn stared out the window, not really seeing the mountains in the distance. "There's a reason people like me have a career. It's because there's a dirty little secret in life insurance." As her mental wheels turned, she started her habitual pacing. "Insurance fraud is easy to commit, and that's why it's such an attractive crime. Pretend I'm . . ."

Hell, what do I call her?

Chels? Chelsea? Ms. Anders?

Finally, Kathryn settled on, "Your ex."

His expression soured. "Oh, let's say you're not."

Not sure if I should be flattered or insulted.

Playing it cool, she continued. "Okay, then let's cut to the chase and say I want to bump you off for a big life insurance payment."

Unimpressed, he snorted. "Harsh."

Huffing through a laugh, she pecked his pouting lips. "I'd need to take out a policy without you knowing. There are a few hurdles, but with a little imagination and the right connections, those obstacles vanish. Okay, we'll jump over the hurdles one at a time. The first one's called insurable interest. Effectively, it means we have a connection beyond being mere acquaintances."

Jake raised his brows. "Is that what the kids are calling it?"

Holding in her giggles, she bit her lip. "Stop."

"But we're not married."

"I did more research. Marriage isn't required to have insurable interest. Even if we're not financially connected, we can establish that interest as long as we're emotionally connected. With spouses, especially in the military, you usually have both. But a fiancée is at the very least emotionally invested."

"Okay, so we've established insurable interest. What next?"

"A few things. Your signature would be required. But a lot of times, in the chaos before a deployment, the insurance paperwork could be slipped in with other paperwork needing your signature. Voila, we have your legitimate John Hancock. Worst-case scenario, let's say I can't get your signature. So I forge it, or have someone else forge it. The problem is that some states require a notarized signature on life insurance policies. But where there's a will, there's a loophole. In this case, notary publics."

Jake squinted at her. "Notary publics?"

"They sound official, but almost anyone can get licensed with little to no effort. The standards for becoming a notary public can be fairly loose, depending on the state. Some states don't bother with requiring training. Others don't even require an exam. Just an application and a few bucks for a seal and a ledger, and *boom*, you're a notary public."

"Seriously? Anyone can be certified?"

"Not convicted criminals, but pretty much anyone else. And nobody ever checks their records. Not that it would matter, because the journal could be chock full of fake data." She shrugged. "It is what it is. But, back on track, I forge your signature and get my buddy to notarize it. In an operation like this, one of two things is likely. I'm forging your signature and notarizing it as myself, or I give my buddy a stack of them and a kickback per signature. I don't know, like fifty or a hundred dollars a signature. If it were me, I'd keep the cash and forge the signatures myself. There's also less risk of a leak."

Jake's uncertain stare stopped her in her pacing.

"What is it?"

He snickered. "I'm really glad you're on our side. Just sayin'."

"Hey, I might think like a criminal mastermind, but I'm determined to use my cold, calculating, greedy thoughts for good."

"Okay, so we've crossed the signature roadblock. What's next?"

"For the next step, a medical exam, we'd definitely need a co-conspirator. I can't just go up to you and say, 'Hey, Jake. Let's get you a checkup. What's that you say? What for? Oh, no reason.' But with you deploying and all, that paves the way for justifying a little probing and prodding. Or, let's say I have a reservist nurse or even a physician in my hip pocket. I can forge everything except the blood tests. For those, I need a reason to physically touch you."

He let out a playful scoff. "So, now you need a reason?"

Laughing, she clarified her position. "No, Kathryn-the-kitten just needs your say-so, and my little claws will be wherever you want them. But Kathryn-the-corrupt-nurse, who's looking to line my wallet with blood money, would need it. At the very least, to run blood tests. But . . ."

Her pacing shuffled to a stop. "What if I called you. Say, I was a medical reservist. I'd have full access to the global directory, meaning I have your number. I'd call, from a base number, with some story about how paperwork got lost, and I need you to come in right away to do additional labs before your deployment. Have you visit my office during the times I'm on duty at the base clinic. You wouldn't think anything of it. Just another waste of time, ticking off another item on an endless checklist before deployment. And I'd look official. You'd be none the wiser."

"So that's it?"

Hands on her hips, Kathryn shook her head. "I don't know. Maybe. Someone would have to pay the premiums until the service member died. And we're talking about a lot of money if all the dots connect. We've got one or more UMOs involved, and for each one of those, we probably have a doctor or a nurse, and possibly a notary public."

Pacing again, she said, "But think about it. If this is going across state lines, who knows just how far-reaching and tangled this web is? And how much money are we talking about? Are underwriters and banking personnel involved? The team already identified over two hundred service members that meet the criteria of being over-insured and on a high-risk deployment. Easily, we're talking about payouts over two hundred million."

Kathryn met Jake's stunned expression, unsure what to say. She grabbed a scrunchie from around her wrist, tempering her growing irritation by collecting herself in a high-and-tight ponytail. It was as close as she'd get at the moment to military bearing.

She had to pull herself together. *Stay focused. Get a step ahead of these bastards.*

Then it hit her. "I think I know how to narrow it down. They're fueled by greed. They might have a certain expectation of a payoff each and every time. What if . . . the service member survives? Returns from their deployment?"

"Well," Jake said as he rubbed his neck, "no payoff, for sure."

"And a risk that the insured will discover someone's taken out a policy on them, even if they don't discover it right away. These policies aren't free, and they're certainly not cheap. Someone has to pay the premiums. If it's the spouse, there's no way big monthly payments to an insurance company would go unnoticed." She closed her eyes for a second and thought. "If I were the evil mastermind, I'd—" She choked back her feelings, but couldn't say the rest.

Jake stood up and pulled her close, saying quietly, "You'd send them back into danger."

Pressing her face against his chest, she nodded. "We can narrow the list by looking for back-to-back deployments." This revelation weighed on her, and she turned to wipe her eyes.

"Hey." He wove his fingers through hers, sealing their handhold. "How about we take a little break after we wrap up today. Dinner tonight, away from here? I'd like to take you someplace special."

"I'm always up for dinner." Her shy smile warmed with the press of his lips.

She headed out, ready to dive back into a few hours of detective work, when she heard him shout, "And pack an overnight bag."

CHAPTER 30

KATHRYN

The closer it got to the end of the day, the more eager Kathryn became for whatever new adventure an overnight bag promised. As the last of the crew left the Russo compound, Kathryn was consumed with Jake's tight-lipped surprise.

He teased her with a hint. "Somewhere off the beaten path, but with great food. Natural, woodsy, but still nice. No evening gowns or anything. Casual. Comfortable. Oh," his expression brightened, "you'll need a bathing suit."

Disappointed, she gave him a frown that matched the knit in her brow.

"Or not," he said with a supremely naughty grin.

Trying to pack, she picked through her limited wardrobe. When Jake had rushed her to his place in the middle of the night, she'd grabbed only the essentials. *And who the hell packs swimwear when they think they're going into protection?* Reconsidering his advice, she answered herself with a giggle.

I guess the answer is "or not."

Jake knocked lightly, waving an Amazon box in his hand. "Delivery for Ms. Kathryn Chase."

"I didn't order anything," she said slowly, a little wary about the unexpected package.

"You didn't? Then I guess I did. Just in case you didn't have everything you needed for our trip. We'll take off when you're ready."

As soon as he ducked out of the room, she tore open the package. Inside were several bikinis in various styles and sizes—and levels of skimpiness. There was even a few sheer cover-ups and some fancy flip-flops. Her inventory of the box led to one revelation.

Jake's definitely not a fan of the one-piece.

She lifted out a string bikini bottom, dancing the scanty scrap of stretchiness before her eyes.

Or very much fabric at all.

With a final swing, she tossed the bottoms into her suitcase, followed by the matching skimpy top. Despite the circumstances, her twinge of excitement climbed to full-throttle giddiness. This was her first getaway in years, and she'd be soaking up every debaucherous moment of it.

~

Kathryn kept her bright smile plastered on the entire time, although the trip had become their own experience with Murphy's Law. Starting it all was Jake's truck blowing a flat on the freeway.

Fixing a flat during the madness of rush hour was a feat in and of itself. But Jake had done it before. What he hadn't done before was dodge golf-ball-sized hail during said tire change. Freak hailstorms weren't an everyday occurrence, but in Colorado, hail happens.

Kathryn suspected Jake's record time in changing the tire would give him bragging rights for years to come.

Next, he'd booked a private executive jet. It was luxurious, complete with leather seats, their own soft blanket-sized pashmina, and stocked with all her favorite snacks and a variety of magazines. She'd never seen anything like it.

It was stunning.

Broken, but stunning.

The replacement part required from maintenance should have taken five minutes. An hour and a half later, they were finally off.

Once they were airborne, Kathryn's motion sickness kicked in. She'd never flown without Dramamine, but it would have taken longer for the drugs to kick in than for the half-hour flight. And the beautiful chocolate-covered strawberries and champagne were just making matters worse.

At least the bathroom was just as stunning as the rest of the plane. She got several really great looks at it. The toilet bowl was remarkably clean. Embarrassed, she apologized to Jake repeatedly.

Between sipping champagne and eating berries, he apologized back for enjoying the spread. But as he put it, "Braving a hailstorm builds an appetite."

The tiny airstrip barely seemed capable of handling their jet. But the plane landed like a champ. A driver with a beautiful black town car waited, ready to take them to their destination. But cell service was sketchy, and several U-turns and dry heaves from Kathryn later, they finally arrived at the Springs Resort and Spa at Pagosa Springs, Colorado.

No matter how many things had gone wrong in the past few hours, everything seemed strangely right to Kathryn. Perfect. Exactly the way a woman who'd been on one deployment after another was used to traveling. A trip filled with one screw-up after another was just her cup of tea.

Like all workaholics, Kathryn had heard about this place, but never found the right excuse to go. She skipped along when they finally arrived, wearing a ridiculous smile, goofy in her giddiness.

"Your mood doesn't spoil easily," Jake said with a grin.

"Crazy as it sounds, days like this take me back. I miss traveling. And it's not just me. You're just as chipper."

He nodded as they explored the property.

When the bright blue of the geothermal spas came into view, Kathryn pulled in an awe-filled breath. "This is gorgeous."

They were overlooking the pristine San Juan River, pocketed with the world's deepest crystal-blue hot springs. Even in the shadows of evening, the lights glistening off the waters shimmered bright, practically inviting her to take the plunge, clothes and all.

The property boasted twenty-four pools of pure mineral water, ranging from eighty to one-hundred-fourteen degrees Fahrenheit. Built by Mother Nature for pure pleasure, the pools were open twenty-four hours a day, seven days a week.

"It's paradise," she said softly, and he squeezed her hand.

"I was hoping you'd have that reaction. I've always wanted to come here, but never have. You're my excuse to drop work. And I couldn't resist the suite we're in."

They arrived at the lobby hand-in-hand, making their way to the front desk.

"Ah yes," the clerk said. "We have you in our magnificent 'O' suite."

Kathryn's eyes widened as she blinked at the clerk, the manager, and then Jake.

With a boisterous laugh, he pulled her close. "It's called that because Oprah stayed there."

Her head sank to his shoulder, hiding her bright red flush as she whispered, "For a moment, I thought it was a different kind of hotel."

Low in her ear, he said, "It is tonight."

Her blush deepened.

Kathryn's appetite was back. With bags dropped off, they headed to the Alley House Grille. They ate and drank as they reminisced, recounting every catastrophe of the day. She laughed so hard, her cheeks ached. Her stomach was full and happy, and sitting across from Jake was one stitch-fest after another. It was as if years of pent-up laughter were all coming out in a single night.

Jake was more than a piece of heaven. He was the hottest slice. Rugged and rough, sweet and sincere, so many complicated layers made up both the Master and the man. A more perfect man couldn't possibly exist. She couldn't imagine being anything but his.

"I need to ask you a strange question," Kathryn said, scooping a bit of Bailey's salted caramel sauce onto the spoonful of chocolate layer cake they were sharing.

"You asked if I thought my hard-on was the same size as my foot, and followed up by asking if you could hold my shoe up to it. Is it stranger than that?" Taking advantage of her distracted laugh, he snatched the spoon of dessert into his mouth, sucking it clean with an exaggerated, "*Mmm.*"

"Hey," she said, playfully frowning at him as she assembled her perfect mouthful again. "There are no strange questions in medicine." She brought the spoon to her mouth, indulging in her own suggestive rendition of, "*Mmm-mmm-mmm.*"

"Watching you eat that spoonful's pretty exciting."

She swallowed, giggling.

Then Jake set her back on track. "Okay, what's your strange question?"

"Um . . ." She stalled, busying herself with fixing the last spoonful. "What should I call you?" She extended the spoonful to him, but he shook his head, pushing it right back to her lips.

"That's all you. And has *Jake* gone out of favor?" His curious grin amplified his confusion.

"I mean," she said quietly, "when we're alone. I've been reading—"

He nudged her hand, lightly shoving the chocolate cake in her mouth. She smiled, enjoying the indulgence and letting him speak.

He moved his chair next to hers. The bright hazel of his eyes darkened, and his voice turned low and commanding. "Close your eyes."

Without thinking, she did. As she waited, her heart raced and her breathing quickened. But nothing was happening. Still, she sat quietly with her eyes shut, trying to quell her nerves by biting her lip.

"There you go again, being disobedient. What did I say about biting your lip?"

That's your job. She pressed her lips together with a wanting sigh.

His whisper was hot against her ear. "I sometimes wonder what would push you to use your safe word. We're in a restaurant. Not packed, but not empty. If I asked you to stand up, you'd do it as quickly as you closed your eyes. I could push you. Insist you bend over the table. What if I pulled up your skirt? Ripped off your panties? Starting with a slow lick . . ."

She parted her lips, saying nothing but taking in a desperate breath.

"You belong to me, kitten, and I'll fuck you wherever and whenever I want."

Trying to utter a word was impossible. Breathing was a challenge.

A second later, his tone lightened. "Open your eyes."

She did, staring at the man she wanted to ride like a pogo stick.

"See, Kathryn? Even without touching you, I control you. Without raising my voice, I command you. I don't care what you call me, because we both know you're mine, to do with as I please, and to please you in ways no one else can."

They exchanged a seductive glance, and Jake called out, "Check, please," just as Kathryn signaled the waiter.

~

Though it was late night, or technically early morning, the idea of taking a sexy dip in a secluded private pool was irresistible. After a quick change into swimsuits topped by bathrobes, Kathryn followed Jake to an oasis of bright blue pools blooming from a sea of darkness.

He sank into the naturally heated spring, but the hunger of his stare didn't rush her. Slowly, she teased her robe down as Jake's eyes darkened. Inch by inch, his heated gaze washed over her body, warming her as she disrobed in the cool wilderness.

"I knew you were evil," Jake grumbled. The mere tone of his voice evoked a shiver that raced across her body. "Remember the rules."

Rules? Puzzled, she searched his eyes.

"If you say *stop*, I keep going. If you say *red*, we stop. But that won't stop me from holding you in my arms and kissing you until I'm satisfied you're all right."

"Oh," she said, smiling through her unusual shyness as she slipped into the water, which was barely waist deep.

He pulled her to straddle him. With his tongue trailing her neck, he tugged at the string holding up her bikini top, caressing her breasts with his hot, wet palms after revealing them.

"This is for you," he said. "Here. Now. Under the stars."

She kissed him, ravenous to taste him.

Hold him.

Love him.

He looked down, staring at the last of the fabric concealing her. "Take them off and give them to me," he said, his voice gruff against her neck.

She untied each side of her bikini bottoms and tugged them away, then placed the scrap of fabric in his waiting hand.

Once he set her suit aside, his hands moved across her thighs, positioning themselves perfectly across her round, firm butt. Then, spreading her cheeks, he rubbed the length of his cock back and forth across her sensitive hole.

Her lips parted, inviting his eager tongue to forage and explore.

Light and tender, he nibbled and kissed her mouth as his fingers grazed her ass. Slowly, he skimmed them back and forth. As his tongue mirrored the movements of his hand, she began to whimper.

She sucked in a breath before moaning louder. Her body took in the slow build of pleasure, ready for anything he would give.

"Hands behind your back," he demanded.

"Here?" Uncertainty rang in her tone as she glanced around, suddenly suspicious of every shadow in the darkness.

"Right here." Low and commanding, he whispered sternly into her ear. "Right now, kitten."

With a terse bite on her earlobe, he forced her hands behind her back.

"Good girl."

Skillfully, he wrapped each of her wrists, tying them snugly but without pain. With her heart beating out of her chest and her nipples peaked and aching for his touch, she couldn't hold back the whimpers underlying each fevered breath.

Slipping a finger between the bindings and her skin, he asked, "Okay?"

Barely able to breathe, she nodded.

His strong palm caressed her breast as his thumb lightly flicked her nipple. Playfully, he scolded her. "Are the bindings okay? Yes or no, kitten?" he said, pinching her nipple hard and releasing her answer.

"Yes," she cried out with a gasp, much louder than intended.

Before her sudden shriek swept her into embarrassment, his mouth was upon hers, comforting her with a deep, soothing kiss.

"Good." Barely at her entry, he thrust deep inside, forcing her tight walls to stretch wide.

She pressed her lips to his neck, quieting her ecstasy in silent shouts. Wrapping her hair around his hand, he pulled her face away to command her.

"Ride me. Hard."

Her body moved to his will as a wandering finger skimmed her skin until it stopped at the sensitive hole of her butt. Working back and forth over his hardness, she obeyed him, riding the fullness of his cock, even as his finger inched in, working its way deeper and deeper into her tight ass.

"Is this what you want? Me, filling all of you at once?"

He didn't wait for a response. A second finger pushed in, stinging and yet soothing, fucking her from behind while his cock worked her core.

"Yes," she said, her voice quivering.

She sucked his tongue as he forced it into her mouth. Her body rocked with all of him, tightening and tantalizing in a swirl of sensations ready to erupt.

"You belong to me," he said low. "All of you."

God, yes. All his.

There was nothing but Jake—everywhere—consuming her with a lustful bliss where nothing mattered but every second of his touch.

His thrusts split her wider. Her body chased a peak of pleasure so intense, she struggled for air. Arching back and shuddering, a series of wild cries pierced the quiet night.

They were her own.

Panting, she collapsed against his shoulder, shaking in his hold. His thick cock pushed deep inside her, pulsing and releasing his own hot climax deep into the center of her core.

Releasing her wrists, he held her, tenderly kissing her cheeks and head. "You're so beautiful, Kathryn. And you're mine."

Once they were robed and ready to head back to their suite, with their wet swimsuits tucked into the oversized pockets of the plush cotton, Kathryn was startled by a member of the staff. He approached, armed with a small-caliber rifle.

"I need to ask you folks to head back to your room."

Kathryn clutched the robe tighter around herself, burning with embarrassment.

Jake played it casual. "Sorry, I thought the pools were open twenty-four hours."

Damn, this man has balls. I mean, bigger ones than my eyes-on verification proved.

"We've had complaints of loud cries . . ."

"Yeah?" Jake said, wrapping a tight arm around Kathryn, securing her to him before she could bolt.

The staff member nodded. "And we've got bobcats and cougars."

Kathryn blew out a relieved breath. "Oh."

Jake squeezed her side as he said, "Well, we heard it too. And it was definitely a wild cat of some sort. My money's on a cougar."

Glaring at him, she suffered the sting of being freshly branded.

∽

Later, comfortable in their luxurious bed, Kathryn sighed as Jake tugged her body close to his. Her head relaxed into its permanent nightly home nestled in the crook of his neck. His free hand stroked through the strands of her damp hair. They both lay there, awake.

"I need to tell you something, Kathryn."

Something in his low tone made her tense, a level of seriousness she hadn't heard from him before. She looked up, studying his expression. "You can tell me anything."

"You sure?"

No, she thought, but she sat up, bracing herself for the unknown impact of something important.

"Yes," she said, confident she could conceal the worry in her eyes.

He sat up as well, and reached up to caress her cheek. "When this case is done, which might be very soon, what are your plans?"

Confused, she asked, "My plans?"

What plans? I've been flying by the seat of my pants since our first night. For the first time in my life, I have no plans.

With nothing to say, she stayed silent.

"Are you going home?" he asked.

She turned away. "I guess . . ."

"You guess?"

Something in his tone rubbed her wrong. *Is he mocking me?*

She looked back at Jake, and his cheesy grin made her collapse with relief in his arms. "Are you messing with me?"

"No, kitten," he said before he kissed her softly. "What I'm doing is making sure you don't have an escape plan. Because if it's up to me, you're never leaving. I've watched you for years, making sure you were all right. Protected. I love you, Kathryn. And I want you to move in with me."

She cupped his face, softly rubbing the stubble on his jaw. "I love you too, Jake."

Their lips met as they melted into each other, clinging to the moment. Again, her body begged for the hard rush of being made his.

CHAPTER 31

KATHRYN

The ride home was the exact same distance as the ride to the resort, but it felt different, flying by so much faster than Kathryn preferred. She held tight to Jake's hand, locked in a fantasy that had become her reality.

As they rolled up his driveway, a word hit her stronger than it ever had before.

Home.

She'd never moved in with a guy. Even with her husband, they didn't move in together until after saying *I do* . . . which undoubtedly contributed to her biggest mistake.

She'd lived every moment of married life as an intruder. The house had been his, and he took every opportunity to mark it. A series of matrimonial missteps made wedded bliss an exhausting, eggshell-walking ordeal.

Her toothbrush should go here.

The cups don't go there.

Although there were two walk-in closets in the master bedroom, they were taken, but she should feel free to use the others around the house.

From the second she'd moved in, divorce loomed closer. And

the road to redemption would be filled with cold, mechanical, snore-worthy sex. For a guy who spent years fine-tuning his knowledge of anatomy, the surgeon extraordinaire couldn't once find her clit. She'd once half considered drawing an arrow pointing to it using a Sharpie.

Jake was the polar opposite—easygoing and fun, with a dark side that made her wetter than a Slip 'N Slide. Their bond was different. Deeper. A connection forged by his blood and her tears, forever binding them.

Jake insisted on a memorable entry into the house. No sooner had she hopped out of his truck than she was flung over his shoulder, butt up and giggling. "God, I love this gorgeous ass."

"My eyes are down here," she shouted from below.

"Pipe down," he said with a strong smack on her cheek. Rubbing her jeans, he reminded her, "I'm not looking at your eyes."

About to head to the stairs, their fun was interrupted by a call. With his phone in his back pocket, he asked, "Mind getting that?"

Upside down, she tugged the cell from his pocket and handed it to him.

"Hey, Scott." Jake clicked it to speaker, then set Kathryn on her feet so he could talk with the detective. "Kathryn's here too."

"Jake, we got a break. A name."

Jake's hand smoothed over Kathryn's shoulder as he responded. "If the name is *Carter*, we've got more investigating to do."

Delaney's irritation came through. "If you're already two steps ahead of us, what the fuck are we doing? Pardon my French, Kathryn."

"I'm an Army nurse, not a nun, Scott. And it's not Jake and his team pumping the brakes. It's me." Kathryn's calm pushed beyond her concern. "I wish I could say more, but it's a very strong hunch." Wincing, she said, "And there's a Carter Reeves who is both military ... and my ex-husband."

"Say no more." Delaney's voice was insistent. "Let's leave it at *you've got a hunch*. Let me know if I can help."

Kathryn let out a small sigh of relief.

Jake pulled her close, tightening his hold with a soft kiss. With a telling gaze, he asked a question. "Since we've got you on the phone, Scott, we're cleared to drop by Kathryn's place so she can pick up a few things, right?"

"I'll do you one better. I'll meet you there. We're done with her car. I can drop if off if you give me a ride back."

"Deal," Jake said, caressing Kathryn's cheek and giving her a tender kiss as he disconnected the call.

~

Kathryn smiled, overflowing with excitement as they headed back to his beast of a truck to drive to her condo. Just a few months back, she'd pretty much written off romance. Before Jake, picturing herself as a spinster with a cat or two, or eight or nine, seemed inevitable.

But with the way his warm hand spread over her knee, any life without his touch would be impossible. Their connection was inescapable, not that she had any reason to flee. Her hand fell gently on his, giving it a lingering squeeze.

At her condo, Delaney was standing beside her HR-V, which was a sight for sore eyes.

As soon as they got out of the truck, Kathryn blurted, "I've missed you."

Delaney's grin was the largest she'd seen. "Well, at least someone appreciates me."

She lifted off the ginormous hug she'd just given her car to pat him on the arm. "I always appreciate my favorite detective."

Instantly, the silence filled with the unspoken questions about Carter. As she struggled to begin a sentence, Jake jumped in.

"Kathryn, how about you grab a few things? I'll catch Scott up.

My guess is he's as glued to the indoors as I am, and the fresh air will do us both good."

She nodded, keeping the PDA to a minimum with a subtle peck to his cheek. "I'll put my car in the garage and grab a few things."

"No rush. Take your time." Between those bright hazel eyes and his dazzling smile, she needed just one more kiss.

The heavy, stale air of the condo hit her. Suddenly, very little about it seemed like the home she'd made for three years. As she passed the bathroom, the eerie feeling that someone had been watching her made her glad she was leaving.

In the bedroom, she grabbed a large suitcase she rarely used, and began collecting her things.

From behind her, she heard a man ask, "Going somewhere?"

CHAPTER 32

KATHRYN

Kathryn looked up at the man leaning against the frame of her bedroom door, his crazed eyes fixed on her, looking her up and down. "Artie? How did you get in here?"

He jingled a pair of keys in front of her face. "I've been waiting for you. For days now. The last time we were interrupted. This time," he held up a knife—the largest from her butcher block, "it's just you and me. And just in case you manage to slip away," he opened his jacket, displaying a gun in a shoulder holster, "I've got you covered."

He doesn't know Jake and Scott are here. Calming herself, she asked, "What do you want?"

His menacing glare moved from her to the knife in his hands. "Don't you know?"

That you're a whack-job stalker? No clue, but you being at both the restaurants I was at should have been a big freaking red flag.

Slowly, she shook her head.

"I want what any man would want. At first, just to fuck you, then kill you. But now . . ." He pressed the knife to the comforter, dragging it down the bed and slicing through the fabric.

Her heart pounding, she said, "You don't have to—"

"You're a hard person to find, even with the military grade tracker I hid in your purse. You kept vanishing into thin air, but you always came back out of your little hiding place. And I was right there. Watching you while you teased me. In your shower. Slowly stripping at that spa. Fucking that guy right in front of me."

"Art, we can—"

"You know what I'd like right now? I'd like you to call me by my name." The flat blade of the knife was at her cheek. "Come on, Kathryn. Let's see how much you've figured out. Everyone thinks my first name is Arthur. But you're too smart for that, aren't you?" His eyes turned cold. "Say it."

The realization was instant, forcing her eyes shut. Her throat dry, she could only whisper, shuddering as she said, "Carter."

"See, I knew you had it. Now, this is why I need to take my time. Which should be fun for both of us, since you're into that, right? Someone tying you up and beating the shit out of you while they fuck you?"

Uncontrollably, her head shook.

He snatched a fistful of her hair, forcing her to meet his gaze. "Do you have any idea what a senior-ranking enlisted man makes in retirement? Pennies," he shouted. "I gave twenty-four years of my life to the military. Been in war zones over a dozen times. Medals upon medals that didn't add up to shit in the real world. But I found the fatal flaw in the system, and the money rolled in. See, I had brains, and a few friends who never had an issue with killing. The way I never had issues with killing."

He let the knife gleam before her eyes. "It's your turn to suffer. You destroyed everything I worked for. Recruiting. Building. Finding the perfect marks. Moving the money. Funding the fucking premiums out of my own pocket. Making sure people died when they were supposed to. Years and years of work. And you, asking people questions, and writing down every word in that fucking notebook." He gripped her hair tighter and yanked at her head. "Where is it?"

The tip of the knife poked through her shirt, pricking her skin.

A loud knock came from the corridor. "Hello?" rang through the condo.

Scott.

The knife pressed, the sharp blade forcing a gasp from her throat as she thought fast. "I left the garage open. They're delivering my new laptop. It needs a signature." When Art hesitated, she shouted, "Just a minute. You need a signature for the laptop, right?"

Silence.

She swallowed hard, forcing every breath in and out.

Come on, Scott. Please . . . you've got to have a hunch. Trust your gut feeling.

A moment later, the voice boomed from the door. "Yes, ma'am. Just a quick signature, and I'll be on my way."

Art's eyes shifted back and forth, as if processing it all. He jerked her arm. "Try anything, and you'll be the reason this guy dies too."

When she nodded solemnly, he released her arm, whispering in her ear, "I'm right behind you."

Delaney stood outside the front door she'd left ajar, wearing his sunglasses and holding a box—the empty laptop box from the last delivery.

Slowly, she approached the door, very aware of the sting of the knife at her side.

Irate, Delaney shifted from foot to foot as he huffed. "Lady, listen I'm trying to be patient, but I don't got all day. Can you sign, already?" When she paused at the cracked door, he looked up as if rolling his eyes. "Seriously, I'm not allowed in. You're gonna have to open this a little wider."

Glancing back at Art, she waited.

Delaney's voice boomed. "Today, lady!"

Art's nudge at her shoulder was all she needed.

The second she pulled the door open wider, Delaney yanked her outside, tossing her behind him as Jake stormed past them into the condo.

Frantic at the scuffle she heard inside, she shouted, "Jake!"

With his weapon drawn, Delaney gave her a stern look as he shouted, "Stay here! Backup's on the way." Then he pushed his way into the condo.

Panicked, she screamed, "But he's got a—"

Her warning was interrupted by the sharp, unforgiving crack of a gunshot.

CHAPTER 33

KATHRYN

There's nothing a former ER nurse knows better than what to expect in an emergency. But none of that had prepared Kathryn for this.

The body does strange things in a state of shock. Hers stayed numb as her hands took over, going through the motions of saving Jake's life. Her reactions and emotions were shut off, allowing her medical training to take over. At least, long enough for the ambulance to arrive.

Knowing too well what would come, her brain ticked off the steps.

Ambulance ride? Twenty minutes.

Surgery prep? Almost no time if the team was ready.

Surgery? She couldn't know for sure. An hour. Maybe two. Damage to the body would dictate that. Bleeding would be a big concern, but could be controlled to some degree with a transfusion.

Other potential variables she considered ratcheted her worry higher—damaged organs, broken bones, spinal impact.

Each breath nearly choked her. Every minute seemed to stand completely still.

And then, there was Art. Barely a scratch on him. Hollow-eyed, his sadistic grin was too much. The bastard enjoyed the pain he'd inflicted, like a sick motherfucking serial killer. She turned away, wholly unsatisfied as the officers carted him off to jail.

At the hospital, Detective Delaney stayed by her side until her friends arrived to take over. Rubbing her hand. Forcing sips of water on her. Being there in a way that had nothing to do with medicine, and everything to do with helping their best friend. But she barely noticed them.

All she saw were the swinging doors that Jake had been taken through. The ones that anyone with news would return from. Unwavering, her stare stayed fixed on them.

And with every blink, visions of his body lurked at the front of her mind. Lifeless. Colorless. Almost . . . *dead*.

Finally, she caved, overcome with all the emotions she'd suppressed. Sobbing, she broke down as her friends huddled around her, comforting her as best they could without a word.

But Jake had been there before, blazing through death's door to return to life. To her.

Come back, Jake. I need you.

CHAPTER 34

KATHRYN

As she alternated between pacing, sitting, and sobbing for an hour, Kathryn finally got some news.

Jake was stable. He'd be unconscious for a while, but the news snapped her from despondent to determined. She had to see him, and ran through the scenario.

The first stop on his long road to recovery would be the intensive care unit. He wouldn't be moved from the ICU until the attending physician felt confident that Jake's vitals would hold.

Heavy sedation was expected after an aggressive operation. So, visiting hours were unlikely at all today. And let's not forget—visits in his condition were restricted to family. But bullshit rules were made to be broken.

She wouldn't exactly be waiting for an engraved invitation but barging down the hallways of a hospital would only get her kicked out.

She needed a plan.

Scrubs and a cap were easy enough to come by, and instantly give her the power of invisibility. But she couldn't move freely without an ID badge, and this wasn't her stomping ground.

She pulled the Kat card, summoning Thelma and Louise, and

they did what BFFs do. Dana handed over her badge, while Laurie walked her through the hospital layout. They hugged Kathryn for luck, and emphasized that if she got caught, they don't know her.

Kathryn breezed through endless hallways and passed half a dozen nursing stations before finally finding Jake's room. He was peacefully asleep, his breathing assisted by a ventilator. Oxygen was being pushed through a tube down his throat, keeping him going until his body was strong enough to take over.

She studied the monitor. His vitals were good, strong for a badass who'd battled death twice. She reached out, examining his morphine line. The drips were steady. She ran a hand down his body as she stepped to the end of the bed where she snagged his chart. The penmanship was atrocious, and she could barely make out some of what it said.

F in penmanship. A+ in surgery. You do you, Doc. And with enough squinting, I'll figure out the chicken scratch.

"Oh, Doctor." A soft voice came from the doorway. "How's he doing?"

Kathryn spun around but couldn't speak. She'd know this woman anywhere, though she didn't know her personally. Her online presence preceded her, though her appearance now was a far contrast from her internet persona. Red-eyed and weepy, the woman entered, dabbing her makeup-free face with a wad of tissue. Ready or not—and Kathryn knew the answer was *not*—she was meeting Chelsea Anders.

Kathryn flipped through the chart in a poor attempt to gather her thoughts. "Uh, he's stable. I'm not his doctor. I'm a nurse."

"Oh."

The ring of disappointment in Chelsea's voice was oh-so-familiar. As if Kathryn's day couldn't get crappier, Jake's ex had instantly relegated her to the B-team because the initials following her name were RN and not MD.

"I was hoping to speak with someone who knew what was

going on. No offense," Chelsea said. When Kathryn stayed quiet, Chelsea picked up Jake's lifeless hand. "Jake, please don't leave me."

Stunned, Kathryn stared at her. *Leave* you?

"Do you believe in second chances?" Chelsea asked, and Kathryn could only stand back with a silent nod. "I can't lose him again. I was wrong about so many things. But I know I can make it right. I just need a chance."

She pulled Jake's limp hand to her cheek, kissing his palm. It was only then that Kathryn caught the glint of Chelsea's engagement ring.

Kathryn dropped the chart back in the pocket at the foot of the bed, freeing her hands to wipe her eyes. About to leave, she was stopped by the doctor entering.

"Oh, no one should be visiting now," the doctor said to Chelsea. "I heard his fiancée was waiting, but I'm sorry, you'll have to go for now. Nurse?"

Reactive and mechanical, Kathryn answered in the role she'd always played. "Yes, Doctor?"

He motioned for her to escort Chelsea out. "We'll keep you informed," he said to Chelsea, "but stay in the waiting room. You'll be able to see him soon. Very soon."

And just like that, Kathryn had been dismissed from the main chapter of her life.

Seeing Chelsea kiss Jake's cheek nearly killed Kathryn. She could only release her breath with the echo of Jake's voice. *Breathe, kitten.*

Keeping up appearances, she passed the doctor, holding Chelsea's shoulders for her own support. Obediently, she led the woman to the waiting room, holding back her own tears as Chelsea sobbed.

"I just saw him. I shouldn't have let him go. Why did I let him go? We're meant for each other. Childhood sweethearts. Engaged.

Our parents are still best friends. Now, everything is such a mess. He was so upset about the pregnancy . . . it was the whole reason he gave me his house. Now all I can think about is him. I just need a second chance. He has to be all right. I need him."

Pregnancy?

Sniffling, Chelsea flashed the ring, more to herself. But Kathryn couldn't help brushing the naked finger of her own hand.

"I put it back on after I saw him," Chelsea said as she dabbed at her eyes with the tissues. "He showed up out of the blue, and it's like nothing had changed. He was back. I saw it all in his eyes. I love him, and I know deep down, he loves me."

At the door to the waiting room, Chelsea pulled Kathryn into a hug, smothering the last ounce of strength from her soul. "Please, please—give him back to me."

For no reason at all, Kathryn hugged her back, an automatic response she'd given a million times before when the friends and family of patients needed it. Pushing aside her own gut-wrenching feelings, she reverted to Kathryn-the-nurse, determined to lift someone else.

Firming her own voice, Kathryn reassured Chelsea. "I will."

∼

After leaving the waiting room, Kathryn took a long, lonely walk back to the ICU. Watching Jake's chest rise and fall as air was forced in and out of his lungs, she stood next to his bed, knowing when he opened his eyes, he'd see the woman he was meant for . . . Chelsea.

Kathryn rubbed his hand. He deserved more than what she could give him. The life he'd known before war had ripped it away. Now it was his turn for a second chance.

He'd been gone so long that night. With Chelsea. Of course

he'd stick by Kathryn. But now, it was as clear as day. He wasn't in love with her. Just . . . indebted.

Sleeping, he stirred, tightening his hand around hers. His grip squeezed every tear from her eyes and ache from her heart. Kathryn licked the salt from her tear-soaked lips and kissed him on the cheek.

She'd never be ready to let go. But she could do this. For him.

Her whisper was soft in his ear. "I'm giving you back your life. I love you, Jake."

CHAPTER 35

JAKE

What happened? Where's Kathryn?
Morphine messes with the mind, but not this much. Something was terribly, terribly wrong.

The more Jake came to, the more he worried. *Did something happen to her?* He scanned the room, realizing he wasn't imagining the person standing next to him.

Chels? What's she doing here?

The news was on, silently broadcasting from a flat-screen TV hanging from the ceiling. Based on the captions scrolling along the bottom of the screen, today was Thursday. *I've been here two days.* A few minutes passed, and the doctor and nurses surrounding his bed explained they'd slowly inch the tube from his throat.

And not a moment too soon. He needed to find out what had happened to Kathryn.

Once the tube was gone, his husky voice strained to push out a semi-coherent thought. He meant to say *Kathryn*, but it came out differently. "Kitten."

Confused, the doctor and nurses looked at Chelsea, who looked back at him.

"Sounded like you said . . . kitten," Chelsea said, and his drugged head nodded. "You want a kitten?"

Her laughter couldn't irritate him more, a high-pitched mix of relief and ridicule.

"Don't worry," she said, "we'll get you a kitten as soon as you get out of here. Just relax. You've got a lot of recovering to do, mister." She rubbed his arm, and his opioid-laden body was alarmingly fine with her hand on him. "And I'm going to be right here by your side."

He mentally repeated her words.

Right here by my side? Did I wake up in the Twilight Zone?

His eyes tracked her as she stood.

"I need to go, but I'll be back." Her lips pressed against his as he tried backing his head further into the firm hospital pillow.

Holy shit, this isn't the Twilight Zone. I've died and gone to hell.

With Chelsea out the door, he managed to move, grabbing the scrubs of the nearby nurse as he struggled to speak.

"Easy. Don't strain too hard," she said. "Voice loss is a common side effect of the tube. It'll come back."

He motioned with his hand, miming scribbling in the air.

"You want a notepad?" the nurse asked, and he nodded with a relieved smile.

He couldn't quite grip the pen she brought him at first, but pushed out the large letters across the pad to write *Kathryn* and then *Chase*.

The nurse shook her head, and he added the word *nurse* before it. Again, nothing.

Nothing?

He had another idea and flipped to a fresh sheet, where he wrote three words: *Detective Scott Delaney.* The nurse shrugged, finally catching on when he added the word *Urgent*.

With a nod, the nurse headed out. "I'll get a hold of him."

Jake had dozed off but jolted awake at the knock at the door.

Scott let himself in. "Hey. If you're sleeping, I can come back."

Jake waved him in, smiling in relief at the sight of his good friend.

"Damn, man. Once a hero, always a hero, huh?" Scott rolled the nurse's stool over next to the bed and sat down. "Don't worry. That son of a bitch will be behind bars for a long time. Hey, they said your voice will take a few days to return, so now I can give you all the shit I want without all the pesky back talk."

Still clutching the notepad, Jake flipped back to the first sheet and tapped the pen to the page, pointing at the word *Kathryn*.

"What about her?"

Desperate, he added *okay* with a question mark.

Scott nodded with a curious lift of his shoulders. "Yeah, I think so. She was here."

Jake's frantic scribbling resulted in a string of all caps. *FIND HER.*

"Okay, okay. No need to yell." Scott hurried out the door, then ducked his head back in. "Glad to see you're better than ever, barking orders like I work for you."

They exchanged a grin before Scott headed out for good.

With the important stuff out of the way, Jake drafted another note. Satisfied as he reread it, he rang for the nurse. Cheerfully, she entered. "Hey there. How can I make your day brighter?"

Jake handed her the folded piece of paper, studying her as she looked it over. The kittens stamped across her scrubs made him smile.

She nodded. "You got it. I'll make sure the staff knows to keep her out." She checked his saline bag and vitals, then flipped through his chart. "Looks like you've declined pain meds for a while. You should really stay ahead of the pain." *Too late.* "Need a little something to take the edge off?" Even pain addicts have their limits. His slight nod was all she needed. With a wink, she said, "I'll be right back."

With a deep sigh of relief, he laid back. At least he could rest easy knowing when he woke up, Chels wouldn't be pawing him.

CHAPTER 36

KATHRYN

The knock at Kathryn's door was demanding. She confirmed her suspicions through the peephole and stayed quiet.

"Open up, Kathryn. I traced your cell signal here."

Dammit. Shouldn't you be chasing bad guys?

After opening the door a cautious crack, she felt like an idiot and pulled it wide open. "Hi, Detective," she said, greeting him with a wary smile. His hopeful expression didn't go unnoticed, and she finally relented. "Come in."

"Should I be offended by the warm welcome?"

Not ready to talk, she was embarrassed when her eyes filled with tears.

He gently touched her elbow. "Hey, Kathryn, what is it?"

She made her way to the couch and he followed, sitting on a chair with assurance in his eyes.

"Jake's all right. He's out of the woods."

Shaking her head, she took a moment to let the tears pour out. He waited until she was ready to talk.

"It's not that." She tugged a few tissues free from the box, dabbing her cheeks and taking a breath into them. "Did you know Jake was engaged?"

Delaney's face dropped. "What? No. I've known the guy for two years. I'm a detective. If he was engaged or even on the verge of it, I'd know. He's never mentioned a woman in his life until you."

"No," she said, trying to explain. "Before his last deployment, he had a fiancée. He had . . . a whole life."

Delaney sighed. "I don't understand."

"Did he tell you who I was?" she asked, and Delaney shook his head. "I'm the nurse who saved his life. He's with me because he thinks he owes me. But he doesn't."

Kathryn dropped her gaze, staring at her hands twisting the tissues in her lap.

"I saw his fiancée. She's still in love with him. And if I wasn't in the way, he'd . . ." She sniffed into the tissues. "If I'm out of the picture, he'll finally get the life that he was cheated out of. And he deserves it. He's been through hell. He's owed his life back. I have the power to make that happen. And I will."

CHAPTER 37

KATHRYN

Twelve days later

The longer Kathryn stayed away, the more she fell apart. Jake was fine. She knew at least that much. And Art was going to prison, with or without her testimony. There was no chance he'd enjoy freedom anytime soon. If he'd pulled this in another state, he'd be looking at the death penalty. And the notebook he was so desperate to get? She couldn't touch it. That a few scribbles could nearly cost Jake his life was too much.

Committed to moving past this all as quickly as possible, she perused the reservist job assignments. At least it kept her away from her phone. She'd shut it off when Jake's texts started rolling in. And voice mails. And emails. Followed by everybody and their mother getting in on giving her advice.

I'm off the grid.

Well, except for the internet.

Frustrated, she skimmed through the reservist openings. The countries were blurring together. For nearly two weeks now, she'd moped around her condo in the worst sort of funk. Nothing would kick her into high gear like getting back into the action. At least, her mind could focus on something other than Jake.

Nursing. Her first love.

Overseas. Far away from sitting around in sweats and crying with her best friends Ben and Jerry. But if she was doing this, it had to be in a country she hadn't been to yet.

In between saving lives, I can see the sights.

The list of endless countries needing nurses trailed on and on.

Afghanistan. Another listing in Afghanistan. Turkey. The UAE. Several countries in Asia. Even Italy. God, it's like the need for nurses tripled since I left.

A knock at the door pulled her from her laptop. Same old knock. But this time, the face in the peephole brightened her day.

There was no use pretending. She was glad to see Delaney for more than one reason. She needed news, especially before saying good-bye to Colorado.

Cracking the door open ever so slowly, she playfully peered through it. "Hey, Detective." Then she flung it wide for him to enter. "Just kidding. Come in."

When Delaney didn't bother going farther than a step in, she said, "I know I shouldn't ask, but how's Jake?"

"Jake? Uh, he's actually the reason I'm here. Listen, we have a situation, and I need your help."

Alarm creased her brow. "Is everything okay?"

"It's hard to explain. But we need to go. Now."

She looked down at the pink flannel pajamas she was wearing. Not exactly ready for prime time. "Sure, just let me change."

Delaney shook his head. "I'm afraid I can't do that. You can grab your purse, and a jacket if you like, but we've got to go."

She grabbed her purse and her longest coat, fashion forward in an ensemble that screamed *bag lady* as she followed him to his car. He opened the passenger side door, letting her close it herself as he raced around to the driver's side.

Seconds later, they were heading toward the freeway.

"Look," she said, "you're freaking me the fuck out, pardon my French. What the hell's going on?"

"Please, Kathryn. This is hard for me too. Just . . . let me do what I need to do."

"Do I need an attorney?"

"No."

"For the love of God, Detective, throw me a bone?"

Delaney gave her an apologetic look. "I can't. I wish I could. Please don't worry. Just sit back. We'll be there soon."

~

After twenty minutes of simmering, Kathryn's freak-out boiled over. As they rolled through the massive gates of Jake's compound, she turned to Delaney. "Is something wrong with Jake?"

The detective stayed silent as he drove up the winding drive to the front of the house. He fiddled with his cell, and a garage door opened.

They got out together.

She was on his heels, racing through the corridor. At the foreboding door with the metal access panel, they stopped, and the detective just stood there.

"What are we waiting for?" she asked.

He gave her an embarrassed shrug. "I don't actually know."

Behind that door, Jake could be hurt. Or just needing her help. Shoving Delaney aside, she pressed her palm to the panel, not knowing what else to do.

Surprising even her, the door unlocked. She couldn't wait for it to open all the way before squeezing in.

"Jake?" Whirling around to the detective, she caught him closing the door but remaining on the other side. "What are you doing?"

"Repaying a debt." Raising his voice, Delaney shouted, "We're even."

The door shut.

"There you are," an irritated voice boomed from the top of the stairs.

She looked up. Despite the scold in his glare, Jake looked better than ever. Gorgeous and brooding, he was the man she'd never stop loving.

"You know," he said as he stalked down the stairs, "after being shot, surviving surgery, and coming back from the clutches of death for a second time, how is it possible that *Nurse* Kathryn Chase was nowhere around?"

His last step toward her was daunting. She took a small step back. Pocketing his hands, with his dark gaze bearing down on her, he waited for an answer.

But she didn't have one. Fumbling for words, she had to look away. Seeing those hazel eyes again burned her tears free.

"You were in good hands," she choked out. "The last thing you needed was a washed-up nurse."

Jake stepped closer. "I see. You stayed away to avoid my exposure to second-rate health care. Of course. Makes sense." Each word was ripe with sarcasm. "Who does that? Leaves someone on death's door without a care in the world?"

The tsunami of tears was coming. She had no other options.

Run.

Kathryn raced for the door and opened it, but his large hand slammed it shut.

She didn't move. His body was too close. Too hot.

Her forehead fell on the cold steel in front of her. "Let me go, Jake."

"Okay." The word was soft but pained. "Answer one question, and you can take whatever car you want. Was it a lie?"

"What?" she asked, avoiding the only question that would set her free.

"All of it. Everything you said. Letting me think you were in love with me."

She suffered silently, unable to speak. It seemed to bring him closer.

His low growl poured over her. "Answer me."

She sobbed through her words. "Jake, you don't owe me anything. You deserve a second chance."

His stern voice softened. "What do you mean?"

"I mean Chelsea. She still loves you. You can have your old life back, pick up where you left off. I won't be in your way."

His breath on her hair made her tremble. "Turn around," he said, but she couldn't move. "Please," he whispered.

She never stood a chance. His demands were her weakness.

Turning around, she kept her eyes down, staring at his body. His shirt looked too soft to hold the body of a man so strong. Beneath it was a fresh wound. One she hadn't had a hand in fixing. A scar she didn't own.

Her eyes shut tight, and she collapsed back against the door.

"Kathryn, I need you to look at me when I say this. Afterward, if you still want to leave, I won't stop you."

Her breathing stuttered, and she finally looked up, sobbing as she met his gaze, which looked as desperate as she felt.

"I will never take Chelsea back, and that has nothing to do with you. She abandoned me, killed our love long before I returned. And she has nothing to do with us. You stood by me, a stranger. The whole world had given up on me except you. You saved me, and for that, I owe you my life. But I could never owe you my love. My heart is a gift, not a debt. In case you have a doubt in that stubborn, selfless, crazy head of yours, I'm madly in love with you. If you don't love me, then you're free to leave. But if you do, then I need to hear you say it—right here and right now—because I am never letting you go. Kathryn, do you love me?"

Weeping, she whispered, "Yes. I'm sorry. I wanted—"

"*Shh*. It doesn't matter. You're here now."

He wrapped his arms around her, kissing her hard before pulling her into a tight hug. A mistake he quickly remedied by releasing her, his wince making her gasp.

"Oh my God, you're still hurt."

Smiling, he stroked a few silky strands from her face. "It's fine. Just recovering from a shot to the chest. Barely noticeable, compared to the unbearable pain of almost losing the love of my life." He kissed her lips again, and again, and again. "Now, how about you stop running away from me, kitten?"

She worked her body under his arm, helping him back up the stairs to the bedroom. "Agreed. How about you stop getting shot, soldier?"

"Ma'am, yes, ma'am," he said, grinning.

She eased him up the stairs and into bed. Tucking several pillows behind him, she urged him to lie back.

When she was just about to snuggle in next to him, he said, "Oh, I don't think so."

His serious insistence took her by surprise, but she understood.

"Of course. You need your rest."

He snagged her hand. "The only way you're getting in this bed is stripped naked."

Smiling, she obeyed. Teasing him, she undressed with slow, deliberate movements.

With a moan, he relaxed back into the soft pile of pillows. "That's it."

Nothing shouted *sexy* like peeling off a thick wool coat hiding pink flannel pajamas. But her man wanted her clothes off, and she was rocking the shit out of this striptease.

Like a showgirl!

In no time, she was buck naked and beaming. She'd never been so happy to shed her clothes in her life. He flipped the corner of the comforter over in invitation, and she scooched in for a kiss, careful of his stitches.

He snatched an elegant gift bag off the nightstand, dangling it before her face. "These are for you."

Inside were two wrapped gifts, one much bigger than the other. She started with the largest, shredding the wrapping in a frenzy of unexpected joy. She propped open the glossy black box. Inside was an eight-piece sleek vibrator set that put her wand neck massager to shame. Some of the pieces were a mystery, but her tingling lady parts were all in.

She recognized the symbol on the label. "Bluetooth?"

"I'm not going to be back to a hundred percent for a month or so. And there's no way you're suffering beside me." He touched the screen of his cell phone and the biggest object in the box shook, vibrating loudly before shutting off. "With a swipe of my finger, your pleasure is in the palm of my hand."

She sighed with a shy smile. "So, I just sit back, relax, and let you do all the work?"

"Only if you know what's good for you." His eyes turned dark, sexy, and sadistic.

Her fingers skimmed across the silicone treasures. Some of the pieces were small, maybe travel-sized. She picked one up, barely bigger than her finger. It was smooth, but not terribly slender. A pretty purple gem sparkled on the end.

"What's this for?"

"Let's just say that I might need to take it easy, but I'm showing you no mercy. I'm taking all of you, kitten. That's what I call the start button."

Biting her lip, it dawned on her she'd been admiring the ornately beautiful pull tab of a butt plug. Her skin warmed at the thought.

"There it is," he said with a growl. "The blush I live for."

It's all she heard. *Live.*

The sweetness of his words pushed her to tears.

His hand cradled her face, softly stroking her cheek. "It's all right. I'm here. I'm fine. And don't forget there's another gift waiting for you."

After wiping her eyes, she pulled a big wad of tissue paper from the bag. Unwinding one lofty layer of tissue after another, she finally uncovered the tiny black velvet box.

"That's my insurance policy," he said, suddenly serious as he opened his hand expectantly.

She placed the box in his palm. "Insurance policy?"

He nodded, giving her a tender gaze. "That you'll stay by my side." With a sexy half smile, he whispered, "Breathe," as he flipped open the box.

I can't. Breathe. Or move. Or believe this amazing man is here. Safe and sound. And all mine.

The fancy diamond ring inside the box sparkled brilliantly, with a color unlike anything she'd ever seen. The twinkling was pure magic. As he slipped it on, it shone like honey in the sun. But then, the light hit it just right, and the color turned a brilliant strawberry blonde.

His dark voice melted her. "Marry me, kitten?"

She could only nod, diving into the sweetness of his kiss. His arms surrounded her, squeezing until an agonized grunt forced his lips away. She pulled back, tearing herself from his warmth.

With a giggle and a tender touch to his chest, she asked, "What should I get you? A bulletproof vest?"

With a shrug, he replied, "Couldn't hurt." He rested back on his pillow. "How about a prescription for sponge baths?"

She nodded, letting another kiss linger. "And a medical massage or two."

His fingers walked across to the box of magic tricks. "Speaking of massages . . ." He pulled one of the vibrators from the pack. "You ran away. And your bad behavior just earned you my wicked wrath. Are you familiar with edging?"

Nervous but intrigued, she softly replied, "No."

His lips curled up, and his eyes were positively sinister.

∼

After a barrage of test drives, Kathryn had ridden the waves of every silicone toy through her valley of bliss, burning up Jake's phone for nearly two hours.

Each time she neared a peak, he backed off, stopping her building orgasm cold until she calmed. Then, he'd nudge her again. He'd driven her out of her mind, edging her closer and closer to what became the biggest climax of her life.

Her exhausted body cuddled into his nude one, with her head lying on his chest. Lulled. Listening. The strong pounding of his heart drew hers closer with every beat.

When I think I couldn't love him more, I hear his heart. And I do.

She was his, the kitten curled up in his arms. Where she'd always belonged.

Just as he was hers.

The toughest man, and the gentlest Master. A wounded soldier always ready to protect. And a Dom who'd fallen madly in love with her.

Eager to give more to the man she would marry, she trailed kisses steadily down his torso.

"Kathryn?"

"Hmm?" Her kisses ended on his thigh, letting her tongue slide up his shaft.

His body tensed. "Is there an insurance policy I don't know about?"

Kissing the head of his cock, she looked up. "You're at risk for blowing a stitch, not having a heart attack. You're not allowed to exert yourself and stretch or strain your wound. But you can have sex. And Nurse Chase will make sure all your needs are met." She licked again, lightly against his balls.

"Stop," he said, a swift command that couldn't stop her for long. Coaxing and sweet, she assured him. "I'll be gentle. I promise."

"Lies will get you punished," he said, grabbing his phone and shooting her the cockiest grin. Something started buzzing, then stopped. It was the box. "Here's how this goes, kitten. We're doing a winner-takes-all round. A battle of wills."

"And what exactly are we playing for?"

"Where we're going on our honeymoon. The person who makes the other come first wins."

She grabbed the box, checking his every advantage. "What are the rules of engagement? Can I use these on you?"

His naughty eyes met hers. "As long as you clear it with my nurse."

Looking him over, she made her decision, grabbing two of the dirty little devils. "And what if we come together?"

He took the box from her, carefully analyzing his arsenal. "That's easy."

After making a few selections, he tossed the box aside and pulled her up for a long kiss.

Breathing slowly with a raised brow, he said, "Best two out of three."

Let the games begin.

Thank you for reading *FALLEN*! I hope you loved meeting Jake and Kathryn. Get ready for the next installment in **RISING**!

A new Dom rises from the ashes.
Not all Doms are made. For Jake Russo, it's second nature.

Kathryn trusts the safety of his hold. She's fresh. She's ready. She was meant to be a sub.

His sub.

It's time to go deeper. Lure her further.
Unravel her with pain and pleasure.
Claim her. Completely.
As her Dom.

Grab RISING Now>>>

∽

Ready for a taste of something a little Ruthless?
Power plays are hard.
Trying to one up the stranger who banged me senseless last night?
Definitely harder.
Available on All Platforms! **Get RUTHLESS WARS Now>**
"Tons of chemistry and passion ... Highly addictive" ~Goodreads Reviewer

∽

Looking for another sexy billionaire?
Meet Davis R. Black ... aka Richard. Some know him as a tech mogul. To Jaclyn, he's the King of the A-holes. Which is why this billionaire is hiding *his* in plain sight. Check out the first book in the Ruthless Billionaires Club.
Available on All Platforms! **Get RUTHLESS GAMES now!**
Flip the page to check out a preview.

∽

Need another fix of steamy suspense? The hot and steamy ALEX DRAKE SERIES with Alex, Madison, and Paco Robles is available on Amazon! **Get ACCESS Now>>>**

When seclusive billionaire Alex Drake sets his sights on Madison, obsession takes over. Unlocking his world was easy. Seducing her was inevitable. But securing her heart might be impossible. He's ready to give in to her every desire except for one. The only thing she wants. An answer. To a tiny question. Why her?

Get ACCESS Now>>>
Read CHAPTER 1

∼

Join Lexxi's VIP reader list to be the first to know of new releases, special prices, and get freebies every week on all platforms!

Free hot romances & happily ever afters delivered to your inbox.
https://www.lexxijames.com/freebies

RUTHLESS GAMES

CHAPTER 1

"Have you ever been obsessed?" he asked.
With the midday sun blazing into his new uptown Dallas office, Richard noticed Margot squinting. He grabbed a remote control. At the press of a button, transparent screens dropped over two walls of windows, softly dimming the sunlight while capturing the panoramic skyscraper views. When her eyes adjusted, she resumed her skeptical scowl.

He couldn't help firing such a pointed question at her. And not just for shock effect. He was revealing a secret truth that no matter how hard he tried, he couldn't escape.

Appearing unimpressed, she stared back. "Players like you don't get obsessed. You get fleeting infatuations, until the next new set of bouncy breasts catch your eye."

He took the jab in stride. Impressing Margot wasn't the goal. Convincing her to join him was. She had a knack for cutting to the chase, a quality he respected.

Facts. Numbers.
All business. No bullshit.
Here we go.

Despite the expansiveness of his fortieth-floor office, they sat a cozy distance from each other, each on a matching tufted black leather sofa, with a low glass table between them. Two chilled Voss waters waited an arm's length away on granite coasters.

The refreshments weren't just there because of the sweltering Texas heat outside. Richard knew the drill. Margot demanded complete sobriety during any negotiation, and this wasn't exactly a social call. With her golden hair perfectly layered in an expensive cut, and a custom suit contouring her svelte body and complementing her delicate features, she was a woman of the world. No doubt about it—her razor-sharp mind analyzed him. Each word. Every move.

And he knew exactly why.

Jumping on this crazy train would take a wish and a prayer, and a butt-load of cash. And crazy wasn't even the half of it.

Illegal? *Definitely not.*

Well, maybe.

Okay, probably.

Richard tried to stay out of anything that was blatantly against the law, but everything about this plan screamed lawsuit. Big, fat, fucking lawsuit. And if the media caught wind of it? He'd definitely be kissing his own ass good-bye. His ass *and* his assets.

He promptly shoved all the risks from his mind, focusing on the ultimate prize. "It's not fleeting. And Jaclyn Long isn't remotely close to a flash in the pan. Any day now, she could take over Long Multinational Systems, and we both know if that happens, it's game over. This is my chance. My *only* shot."

When Margot's gaze remained unimpressed, he decided to change tactics. *Bring out the big guns. Honesty.*

"I'm used to women looking at me a certain way," he said. "Like a gift-wrapped lottery ticket they want to unwrap with their teeth. Half the time they see me as a sugar daddy, and the other half as a baby daddy. But when Jaclyn looked at me, it was different. Like I wasn't worth her time. But she's definitely worth mine."

Margot's brow lifted.

"Here." He opened the folder on the coffee table between them and handed her a few documents. "I'm ready to hit her with all I've got, but she can't see me coming."

Margot skimmed the pages, her smile spreading wider as she flipped page after page.

"You've known me a long time, Margot. If I'm in it, I'm in it to win it. But I need an advantage. You're one of the few people who live in her inner circle."

"Lived," she said, correcting him as she returned the documents and resumed her stoic expression. "It's been a while."

Her practiced poker face made it impossible to get the slightest hint of where she stood. But she was listening, and his instincts kicked in, prompting him to hit the "schmooze" button.

"But you know Jaclyn better than anyone," he said. "Maybe better than she knows herself. To make this work, I need you on my side."

Margot looked up for a second, contemplating a response. Sinking back into the fine leather, she crossed her legs and stretched an arm along the low back of the couch. "And exactly what's that shot worth to you, Richard?"

Well, that was fast. He figured she'd at least hear him out on the details of this scheme. But, nope. She was ready to decide if she was in or out, and it all came down to price. Her casual indifference telegraphed that she knew his position as well as he did. Without a lick of leverage, why pretend?

Richard leaned forward, resting his elbows on his knees. "How about we cut to the chase? Name your price."

She smiled, its immediacy killing any hope he had for a fair and reasonable negotiation. "*Whether* you pull this off or not, I get five percent of your company."

His eyes popped. Margot's hardball game wasn't just in a league all its own. It was like she'd invented the fucker.

He opened his mouth to counter, but the subtle lift of her elegant hand stopped him cold.

"That's nonnegotiable," she said. "And I'll need to see it in writing today. I'll also need five million in good faith money deposited to one of my accounts. Nonrefundable. My attorneys will draw up the paperwork to ensure there's no way I'm implicated if anything goes awry with this 'foolproof' plan of yours. Because what could possibly go wrong, right?"

Her sarcasm was cutting. She reached for a bottle, delicately unscrewed the cap, and sipped, letting him mull it over.

He pulled in a breath. "How about—"

"Nonnegotiable, Richard. I'm not the one who's obsessed."

Their eyes met, and hers sparkled with the triumph of a woman who knew she had him by the balls.

Margot didn't wait for his reply. "Good. Then there's the issue of your appearance."

"Hang on. A ten-thousand-dollar suit isn't good enough for Your Highness?"

She shook her head. "Oh, it's great for me, but I'm not the one you have to worry about." She swept a hand to indicate his appearance. "*Her* Highness will see you coming from a mile away. No wonder she avoided you like e. coli. Guys like you swarm her in droves. Hot. Charming. Sexy, with a naughty side that keeps girls coming back for more."

Richard gave her a not-so-modest grin.

"Absolutely worthless," Margot said sharply, quashing his smile. "Like you rolled off the latest playboy cookie-cutter assembly line. Guys like you have burned her a few times too many. So, if you want this to work, then you're going to need to make a few changes."

Damn her. Margot was enjoying this a bit too much.

He crossed his arms casually over his chest, barely wrinkling the custom-made suit. "Fine. We can work on wardrobe. What else?"

She set down her water and moved to take a seat by his side. "Hmm." She scanned his face. "I'm not partial to facial hair for this little caper."

His hand protectively flew to his scruff, and he rubbed it thoughtfully. The trademark of his signature look, gone?

"Okay. Fine. It'll grow back," he said. "Any more changes?"

She tilted her head, studying him. "I definitely see you as a blond."

Tall, dark, and handsome Richard stripped down to a squeaky-clean choirboy? He hated everything about it.

But he had to admit, the idea was bizarrely genius, and exactly what he'd asked for. Jaclyn Long would never see him coming. Literally.

Richard sighed. "All right. Fine. I'll get my stylist on it."

"Try to get it as close to my color as possible. So people might mistake us for siblings." Margot ran her fingers through his thick hair, uncharacteristically playful as she deliberately tousled his perfectly gelled waves.

Scowling, he pulled away and stood, quickly smoothing back his hair as he crossed the room. He picked up two boxes from his desk and returned, handing her one.

Margot's eyes widened the slightest bit. "I do love gifts." She popped open the box and pulled out a card.

"Scan that. It will load an encrypted app to your phone that works like FaceTime. Then, it's just a quick click to communicate with me through these." He opened the other box and pulled out a pair of titanium-framed glasses, then slid them on.

"Oh, I like those. They make you look even less like yourself."

He frowned. "Nice. And I love how looking less like myself somehow became the goal. After spending the better part of a decade honing my image, I thought I'd be seizing the day in style. But, for what's on the line, consider it done."

"And one last thing, Richard." Margot's usually stoic demeanor turned cheery. "No lies."

Confused, he cocked his head, wondering how she'd missed the gist of the entire conversation. "Uh, that might be an issue, Margot."

Her lips twitched with the smallest of smirks. "You can only take this game so far, and every sport has rules. Your name will be a mystery, and your makeover will be epic, but absolutely no lies. Nothing that can ever be used against you later—in a court of law or otherwise. Lies are too hard to keep up with, and nine times out of ten, they'll bite you in that Adonis backside of yours. You'll look and act the part of an altar boy, but that devil in you will swear to tell the truth. Maybe not the whole truth, but nothing but the truth."

She lifted her bottle for a toast. "Deal?"

He grabbed his water bottle, removed the cap, and clinked it against hers. "Deal. To the future."

"The future."

CHAPTER 2

Three guys walked into a bar . . . It had all the makings of a lame joke.

From her perch on her stool, Jaclyn used the art deco mirror hidden behind the mountain range of booze to inconspicuously spy. People-watching, she loved. Having them watch her back, not so much.

A recovering insomniac, she'd made her way down to the basement tavern at the Joule Hotel desperately needing to unwind enough to get a few hours of sleep. A nightcap wrapped in the soothing ambience of peace and quiet gave her room to breathe. Sneaking in at 1:00 a.m., not long before closing time, usually gave her all the privacy in the world, but not tonight. The inebriated band of makeshift brothers who'd just walked in promised to interrupt her laid-back plans.

She studied the trio as they found a nearby table to ogle her from. By their middle-school glances and huddled and hushed chatting, something was brewing, and it smelled all too familiar. She'd suddenly become the grand prize at the end of a pickup line.

Her thick, wavy jet-black hair that trailed clear to her ass always had a knack for catching wandering gazes. Never accused of being rail thin, Jaclyn had ample assets and voluptuous curves with a magnetic pull all their own. Add to that her bulging bank account and seductive spontaneity, only three types of men ever seemed to plow into her life.

First, there were the money-hungry, status-chasing Ivy Leaguers who pursued her like an Olympic gold medal—as if their years of hard work pinnacled in such a worthy award. These trophy hunters loved the chase, not only to capture and keep such an exotic specimen of woman, but to cage her as well. Like with all confident, capable women, captivity clashed with her charisma.

Taking second place were the uninteresting, unintelligible, garden-variety Neanderthals who traveled in packs and swarmed her in droves. They were less interested in her money and more drawn to her milkshake. Brainlessly so. Despite her best efforts to bind those babies down, her double Ds always brought the wrong sorts of boys to the yard. And this band of bar boozers plopped squarely into this bucket.

But option number three was her weakness. The consummate looks-so-good, feels-even-better bad boy. The edgy kind of guy who wasn't the right fit, but it never deterred her from forcing that puzzle piece in. Deep, deep in.

Ideal for the occasional tawdry and tantalizing tryst, they were perfect in the heat of the moment. It was those disappointing minutes afterward that always burst her bubble. For these good-time guys, both their heads had the attention span of an egg timer.

Even if she could grab their focus, she could never keep it. Sure, the sex was smoking hot. But after spending ten or twenty minutes satisfying his, um, ego, what more was there to do? Even if the owner of the down-and-dirty hot body could carry on a conversation, they rarely did. She'd succumb to the eventual boredom, and they'd be on to their next Betty. The blazing-hot boy-toy trail had become one buzzkill after another.

She watched in the mirror as the men across the room metaphorically drew straws for who would belly up to the bar beside her first.

Feeling frisky, she set her sights on a good time. Her way. And not in an annoying, pissed-off sort of spirit where her bitch face preceded her words. She had way more creativity than to waste her energy on irritation. After a long couple of days at work, a round of lighthearted entertainment seemed just the ticket to blow off a little steam.

These guys were overpreparing to the nth degree, and her mind and mood were ready to roll out the welcome mat. Between their clustered discussion and round of locker-room fist bumps, these chumps promised a few rounds of priceless stress relief.

The first of the three, who'd be the alpha if he could spell it, strolled over with his slicked-back hair, chiseled good looks, and smug grin. "Hi, sexy. Can I buy you a drink?"

God, if there was one thing Jaclyn loved, it was when d-bags didn't disappoint. She smiled adoringly, fully sizing up every arrogant inch of him.

"Well, I was just drinking water." She walked her fingers across the lacquered wood before smoothing her hand over the back of his. Her thick, come-hither lashes batted as she peered through them. "Can I ask you a question?"

He tucked his index finger under her chin, using the opportunity to flex his bicep in a shirt that was clearly two sizes too small. "Anything, sexy."

She was sure the octave of his voice just lowered. *I guess his balls just dropped.*

With a coy smile, she wrapped her hands around his taut arm. "You're *so* strong. I'll bet you play sports, right?"

He nodded, daring to brush her hair off her shoulder, caressing her arm with his rather rough hand.

Dammit, this gorilla is snagging my blouse. She wriggled out of his grasp but leaned forward, knowing the length of his stay, like his manhood, wouldn't be long.

"Well, I was thinking you'd be the perfect man. I mean, for my kids. I have five."

His face fell as he leaned back. But he wasn't getting away just yet.

She grabbed one of his grubby paws, yanking it to palm her stomach. "And one on the way!"

It was like watching a tug-of-war as he tried to get his hand back from her two-fisted grip.

"Hey, what are you doing now?" she asked innocently. "Would you like to meet them? And maybe stay till breakfast? My babysitter is about to bail, and you look like you'd be great with them. Especially the twins. Their sleep pattern is all kinds of off, and I really need some z's."

It was just the reverse pickup line to shrivel his tail. He bailed without a word.

What, no good-bye? She turned back toward the bar and watched through the mirror as he encouraged contender number two, who was now looking her way.

Contestant number two, come on down!

Strolling up, what this guy lacked in a buff bod he more than made up for in a suffocating cloud of Axe body spray.

Curse that company for making an aerosol.

He plopped on the seat next to her. "Excuse me. I couldn't help but notice you from across the room. I mean, that outfit really looks hot on you." He leaned in. "How about I buy you a drink? What can I get you?"

What do you know? He's a closer.
Well, two could play at that game.

Jaclyn settled on a more direct approach. Despite his best

attempt at bravado, his bouncing leg and inability to hold eye contact revealed his nervousness. She swiveled her bar stool toward him, crossing her legs and giving him a front-row view. Her shapely calves and lower thighs poured from beneath the hem of her skirt.

"Well, maybe." Leaning in and letting her breasts test the buttons of her blouse, she pitched her voice in a breathy and demanding tone. "The last guy I dated could hold an erection for two and a half hours, cock ring and Cialis free. God, what I wouldn't give for a long, steady pony ride."

She put her hand on his tapping leg, stopping the bouncing dead in its tracks. "I'm game if you are, stud, but you will be judged. And bound."

He stumbled off his stool and scurried back to the pack.

What about my drink? Oh well.

Next!

As bachelor number three casually strolled her way, he did something unexpected. He connected with her in the mirror, his bright blue gaze locked and loaded on hers.

Men were usually too busy gawking at her assets to make real eye contact. She wasn't quite sure what to do with him, a rare breed of classic guy-next-door that she thought didn't exist outside of sitcom reruns and Hallmark movies.

There was something about him. Magnetic despite his demeanor. She just couldn't put her finger on it.

The way he looked at her. Carried himself. Brimming with casual comfort. Like she could drop by and ask him to mow her lawn, and he'd do it. And whether "mow her lawn" was code for taking her in a hot hour of ecstasy or actually trimming the grass outside her house, she could oddly see him diving into either scenario.

Please don't reek of cheap cologne.

At the bar, he barely tapped the seat next to her, asking politely, "May I?"

Jaclyn took the opportunity to get a better look. The glasses were a poor disguise for an obviously gorgeous man. He reminded her of a blond Clark Kent. How the hell Lois Lane never saw the sizzling hottie behind the thick-framed spectacles was beyond her. She also noticed his suit was nice, but hardly a Tom Ford fit or expense. It hung on the body of a well-built but not overly made-up man.

"Why not? Everyone else has."

Playing this one a little cooler wasn't exactly planned. More like a desperate measure to cover for how hot she was getting. *Like gazing into the sun.* She tore open a straw to sip her water, hoping to quell the blush rising up her face.

He sat on the stool and leaned closer, keeping his back to the two men watching. "Listen, I'm sorry about this, but those guys and I sort of made a bet on who could buy you a drink."

"Oh. I was wondering about all the action I was getting tonight. I figured the billboard I took out in the men's room was finally paying off." She trained her eyes forward, pretending interest in the bar's bourbon selection.

"I'll go. Again, I'm really sorry."

He swiveled to leave, but stopped as she softly said, "Hang on." Perusing the shelf of enticing glass bottles, she asked, "What's the wager?"

He loosened his collar a bit before answering and slowly blew out a breath. "Five hundred dollars."

"Each?" Jaclyn's lip curled up in amusement. "So, I assume if you buy me a drink, I get half, right?"

A glimmer of hope rose in his tone. "Um, yes. Of course."

She tapped her fingernails against the cool wall of the water glass, drawing a fingertip through a few drops of condensation. "I have an idea. Why not go back to them, say you thought about it, and I seemed ready to accept, but you got cold feet. Nervous."

"Nervous? To buy a woman a drink?"

"I don't know. Worried I might expect more. And you're

misleading me. Wing it." She bit her bottom lip. "See if they'll take the bait."

"Bait for what?" he asked softly, questioning her reflection.

She spoke to the mirror, keeping her voice low. "The bait to up the ante." She slipped the straw to her lips, sucking another sip through her confident smile.

He leaned in, shoulder to shoulder, speaking in dramatically hushed tones. "So, you want me to hustle them?"

"Mm-hmm." Her coy look caught his.

"Before I dive headfirst into the short con of a mastermind, can I at least know your name?"

Can you at least tear off your tie? "Jaclyn."

"Richard," he said, then headed back to the huddled men who'd just become his marks.

Jaclyn watched, impressed as he really seemed to be milking it. She was nearly giddy, inwardly cheering him on as his animated chatter continued. Between their insistent nods and his "oh no, I couldn't possibly" posture, her anticipation flipped to elation at the sight of them shoving cash into his hands.

She faintly heard, "Yeah, if you get this, you've earned it."

He quickly tucked the cash in his wallet and walked back to Jaclyn in a decidedly cocky, almost pimp-walk manner.

"Well, Mr. DiCaprio, what are you up to?" she asked as he reclaimed his seat.

He again leaned in, a bit closer than the last time. The man smelled wonderful. A blend of subtle cologne, a freshness that must be his laundry, and an undertone of something that could only be described as him.

"Feel free to call me Leo, and we're up to two grand. I'm really hoping I can buy you a drink now, because I'm on a double-or-nothing deal with these guys. I'd really hate to be out four grand for the short pleasure of your company."

The blue of his softly pleading eyes sent her thoughts straight south, making her wonder if he tasted as good as he smelled. She looked over to see the bartender watching, wide-eyed and curious for her answer.

"I guess you can buy a girl a drink."

The bartender breathed a loud sigh of relief, causing both her and Richard to laugh.

"I'll take my usual, Jim."

The bartender nodded. "And for you, sir?"

"I'll have what she's having."

The bartender handed them two tumblers of Kentucky's best bourbon, and they clinked a toast.

Jaclyn sipped hers, thoroughly enjoying the aroma before letting a "mmm" escape on the exhale. Her coconspirator, on the other hand, took a sip, then desperately tried to muffle the choking that jerked to a cough.

"You okay?" she asked as she patted his back. Her patting turned to petting before she yanked her hand back. *Damn, he's built.*

"Yeah, fine," he said in a gruff voice, clearing his throat.

The bartender handed him a water, and he took a grateful sip.

"So, you're Richard. Richard what?" she asked.

The question seemed to catch him off guard. He straightened his tie. "Would you believe Smith?"

His question of an answer tipped her to annoyed. "Smith. You don't say. What a coincidence, that's my name too."

"Really?"

She glared at him. "No." *Idiot.*

"Too bad." He sipped his remorse away. "Jaclyn Smith will forever be my favorite angel."

Mine too. "What's with the mystery, Mr. *Smith*?"

"I, um . . ."

Her silence spoke volumes while she waited for his response.

He shrugged, finally babbling out, "Well, I mean, you're here late. Really late. And you must frequent this bar regularly enough, because the bartender knows what you drink. And by how this all went down, I guess . . ." He ran a finger along the smooth edge of the bar and sucked in a breath. "I'm just not sure if you're, uh, a . . ."

She whipped her head toward him, her eyes blazing while he fumbled his explanation. "Oh my God. You think I'm a prostitute?"

More shrugging of his broad shoulders as he struggled to smile.

"Just to be clear, *unlike me*, I'm pretty sure a hooker would let anyone buy her a drink. In fact, the three of you would qualify under the call-girl definition of 'the more the merrier.'"

Richard actually seemed to blush. "No, of course not. I never imagined you were, um, a working girl. It's just that I'm, um—"

"Married?" she asked, disappointed. Though by the looks of his left hand, a ring had never graced his finger, as it was smooth. No signs of a tan line or indentation.

"No," he said with a slight huff of indignation. "I'm definitely not married. Look, I'm just digging the hole deeper, and as cool as our little scam has been, I've got to work in a few hours. I need to get going. How can I discreetly hand you half of this wad of cash before I head out?"

Oh, I'm not done playing with you, Mr. Smith.

He'd barely tugged the smooth leather wallet from his back pocket before she slid her hand around his forearm. Hopping off her bar stool, she energetically yanked him off of his.

"Oh, I know a way. And bring your drink."

With his newfound fortune, he left a C-note on the bar.

Leading him along, Jaclyn glued her body to his. It was nothing to fake a conversation punctuated with over-the-top giggles as they passed the two other men. Overtly flirting, she pressed her breasts against him as they strolled out to the lobby and toward the elevators. When the doors opened, she shoved herself against him, backing him inside.

The doors shut.

CHAPTER 3

Once the elevator doors closed, Jaclyn pressed the button for the twentieth floor of the West Tower, and promptly declawed herself from her full-on man attack.

Silence filled the small space as they were whisked upward. A chime announced their arrival. Richard stepped forward to exit, but she snatched his elbow, easing him back.

"Whoa there, cowboy." Again, she pushed a button, this time hitting the one for eleven. The doors closed. "In case your friends check the elevator, I want them to think we're going to my room. We're going to keep an eye out until they leave. I've got a great spot for spying."

"Somehow, I'm not surprised. And they're not my friends."

The doors opened to the famous eleventh floor "rooftop" pool. Touted in travel magazines as an architectural feat, the pool was nestled on a roof of a shorter tower, flanked by the taller twenty-story towers.

Round-the-clock access to the secluded venue offered a private oasis at the moment. Shimmers from the backlit water played perfectly against a backdrop of multicolored city lights and a warm, sweet-scented breeze.

They strolled to the far end of the inviting crystal-clear water, looking out over a glass half wall to the empty street below. Waiting on the undynamic duo's departure was taking forever. With a half-hidden yawn, Jaclyn plucked Richard's glass from his hand and poured his remaining bourbon into her lowball, then set his aside.

He smirked. "Sure, help yourself."

She sipped. "The last thing we need is you choking to death because you can't handle your booze. In a way, I'm saving your life."

He leaned an elbow on the glass railing, fully facing her. "You know, there's an old proverb that says if you save my life, you're entrusted to care for it."

Amused, she mirrored his stance. "Well, the way I heard it is if I save your life, you're now indebted to me for the rest of yours."

His eyes were pure playtime, teasing her with a knowing glance. "I'm actually prepared to accept your terms. Shall we put it in writing, back-of-the-napkin style, or are you as good as your word?"

"Oh, I'm so much better than my word." She tasted her drink, swallowing and letting the heat of the bourbon slide slowly down her throat.

Their gazes locked, and seconds ticked by.

Is he going to kiss me or what?

"So," Richard said, "are you sure they're not guests? Maybe they're going back to their rooms." He looked at his watch. "And as much as I'd love to grab a poolside chaise and glamp, I really do need to head out soon."

Guess not.

Lifting her gaze from his lips, she eyed him up and down. "I know they're not guests like I know you're not a guest, but for different reasons. Your pals were on an obvious late-night pub crawl, checking out the best Dallas bars have to offer, and the Joule is world renowned. They were wearing shirts with the same logo, for a convention that's hosted at the Gaylord. They've been taking their time going from one place to another, not overly drunk, but also not exactly sober. Trust me, they're not staying here."

Richard looked over the edge, studying the architecture of the pool overhanging the sidewalk below. Distracted by the antigravity feat, he seemed totally engrossed in something other than the hot-and-bothered woman standing inches from him.

Jaclyn wasn't sure he'd caught a single word she'd said until he asked, "What about me?" His dazzling blue gaze returned to her. "How do you know I'm not a guest?"

Echoes rose from the street below of men being a little too loud for two in the morning, and Richard and Jaclyn both popped their heads over the railing to see her prediction materialize. The men were leaving the hotel, still jovial, although they must have been kicked out after last call.

"See?" she said smugly. "Not guests."

Nodding, he conceded her point. "You were right. But you're probably used to that."

They exchanged smiles that promised more, and started walking slowly back toward the elevator.

"And me?" he asked.

"You? Take a look at yourself," she said, and he gave himself a quick once-over. "You're still in a suit and tie, likely burning the midnight oil. Then you decided to get away, maybe walk away to refocus. But thinking you'd be back quickly, you didn't bother changing into something casual, as if you're used to wearing suits like a second skin. And, if you were a guest, you would have gone somewhere else. My hunch is that hitting a bar wasn't exactly on your mind, because you don't strike me as the type to drink your way through a puzzle. Well, that and I've seen you drink."

Richard rolled his eyes at that.

"With your obvious workaholic tendencies, alcohol wasn't on

your agenda, or you would've raided your own minibar and dove right back into whatever was bothering you. So, how'd I do?"

He unbuttoned his jacket and pocketed his hands. "I'm staying at the Crescent Court. But this crazy pool caught my eye when I drove in. It's not every day you see a pool hanging over a street midway up a hotel. I had to check the place out."

"At one in the morning?"

His lips lifted in a half smile. "I get restless, and I don't need much sleep. I like staying in big cities because wandering clears my head, and I can blend into the nightlife. You're right. I was trying to wrap my head around something. I happened to come in when those guys did, and, well, I saw you. We *all* saw you."

The deepening blue of his eyes held hers. "You said hello to the folks at the front desk, asking one of them how he was doing with a new baby in the house."

His endearing grin spread a little wider. "Then you made your way to the basement bar, and, looking the way you looked at this hour, we couldn't exactly not follow you. They noticed me noticing you and proposed a friendly bet. Worst-case scenario, I paid a high price for a little entertainment. But I figured I had nothing to lose. I was pretty sure you weren't falling for one of them. And if you did, I probably dodged a bullet." When she gave him an admonishing look, he shrugged. "Come on, you met them."

Truth.

"And best-case scenario?" She skated her fingers back and forth across the railing.

"Well, the wad of cash wasn't terrible," he said jokingly, and she was too charmed to be peeved. "That and I'd get to spend one of my first days in Dallas getting to know a beautiful fellow insomniac."

"So beautiful that you gave me an alias when you were perfectly teed up to hand me your business card," she said, raising her brows.

He gave her a sardonic smirk. "Yeah, why would anyone need an alias around a woman who looks the way you do, and just swindled a couple of strangers out of two grand?"

"I did no such thing." Pretending to be offended, she tapped his chest. "You did all the swindling. I just sat there."

He hung his head for a second, chuckling. "Fair enough. I guess you were just my con-artist life coach. Anyway, I wasn't sure if it was a good idea if we, well, continued—"

"Our mad partnership of crime and mayhem? Fine, I'll start my syndicate solo. Two thousand dollars *and* you got to buy me a drink. Clearing your head seems to be working for you."

She could only hold his gaze for a few seconds before he looked away.

"Oh, speaking of . . ." He pulled out his wallet and fumbled to remove their take, diligently separating it from the cash he came in with.

Jaclyn had just enough time to sneak a peek at the name on his driver's license encased in a clear plastic pocket of his wallet. Reluctantly, she stepped to the elevator and pushed the UP button as he counted the money.

He handed her half. "Here you go. For whatever it's worth, thank you. This was unexpected. And fun."

She eyed the money indifferently, then clasped her hands around his, securing the loot in his grip. "It's yours."

His intrigued baby blues fixed on her as a ping sounded, announcing the arrival of the elevator.

"The pleasure was all mine, Richard. Richard *Austin*." In a final impetuous act to close out their antics, she stole a swift, deep kiss.

His arms had barely molded around her before she pulled away. Admiring the bright red stain now covering his lips, she giggled. His wide-eyed fascination was priceless.

Damn, I'd love to bring Luke Skywalker to the dark side.

She stepped into the elevator and turned to him, sipping her stolen bourbon as the elevator doors closed. A smile tipped up her lips as she watched him standing with his mouth agape, still holding out his cash-filled hand.

∽

Download the first book in the Ruthless Billionaires Club.
Available on All Platforms! **Get RUTHLESS GAMES Now>>>**

ACKNOWLEDGMENTS

To the love of my life, Mr. E. I've never known a man who could be so remarkably rugged and strong, yet so romantic and kind. You are one in a billion. My perfect soul mate.

To my family. It's such a gift to be so unconditionally loved and supported. Your daily calls to 'Betty' always make me double over in laughter.

To the remarkable and insanely talented Pam Berehulke. I am humbled to work with you. Thank you for once again giving my Cinderella words a Fairy Godmother's touch.

To Crystal (and Brad, and the kids, and Maverick). I can't thank you enough for always being there no matter how wild the ride gets. You are amazing!

To my phenomenal ARC readers. I can't even express what it means to have each and every one of you on my team. You are, without a doubt, the sexiest readers in the world!

To my social media family – from Facebook to Twitter, Instagram to blog spots. Your friendship and support continue to make every book possible.

And a very special thanks to my readers from every corner of the world. I'm grateful beyond words.

Love Always, Lexxi

Fallen

Formerly published as Fallen Dom

Copyright © 2020 Lexxi James, Ltd. All rights reserved.

www.LexxiJames.com

Editing by
Pam Berehulke
Bulletproof Editing
https://www.bulletproofediting.com

Independently Published

Cover by Book Sprite, LLC.

No part of this publication may be reproduced, distributed, or transmitted in any form or by any means, including photocopying, recording, or other electronic or mechanical methods, without the prior written permission of Lexxi James, Ltd. Under certain circumstances, a brief quote in reviews and for non-commercial use may be permitted as specified in copyright law. Permission may be granted through a written request to the publisher at LexxiJamesBooks@gmail.com.

This is a work of fiction. Names, characters, places, and incidents are the product of the author's imagination. Specific named locations, public names, and other specified elements are used for impact, but this novel's story and characters are 100 percent fictitious. Certain long-standing institutions, agencies, and public offices are mentioned, but the characters involved are wholly imaginary. Resemblance to individuals, living or dead, or to events which have occurred is purely coincidental. And if your life happens to bear a strong resemblance to my imaginings, then well done and cheers to you! You're a freaking rock star!